DIS

The Manuscript

Rebecca Laskowitz

The Manuscript. Copyright © 2010 by Rebecca Laskowitz.
Printed and bound in the United States of America. All rights reserved.
No part of this book may be reproduced in any form or by any electronic or mechanical means including information storage and retrieval systems without permission in writing from the author, Rebecca Laskowitz, except by a reviewer, who may quote brief passages in a review.

Library of Congress Control Number: 2010932569

ISBN-13: 978-0-9794451-4-9 (pbk.)
ISBN-10: 0-9794451-4-0 (pbk.)

A Story Institute Publication
www.storyinstitute.com

FIC
LASKOWITZ
R

Dedicated to

my parents,

Ben and Lainie Laskowitz

Amie and Russ Riva

PROLOGUE

Up until a few weeks ago, Vincent's life had been about studying, writing, and book signings. His life revolved around his work and his fame. He never thought it would lead to this. Now, the only thing about his life that he truly cared about was keeping it from ending. This was a battle he would lose very soon.

I'm like Jesus on the cross, he thought. Not even at death's door would his uncontrollable ego subside.

Vincent collapsed into his leather armchair as he tried to control his breathing. His breaths came in quick, punctuated gasps as the tightness in his throat increased. Despite the cool sixty-six degrees at which he kept his office, sweat dripped down his temples. A six-foot tall man who surpassed the 300 pound mark had no trouble making his own heat.

Pictures in gold frames made by artists Vincent didn't know, except by price tag, covered every wall of the one place he could usually find solace, his office. This was the one place to which he could return and feel secure. Where there wasn't a picture hanging, bookshelves took up the rest of the wall space. This room—this sanctuary—with everything Vincent considered important and meaningful, could not save him from the inevitable outcome of his predicament. He placed his hands on the armrests and clenched his fists into tight balls as the reality of his situation sunk in.

The Manuscript

Vincent wasn't used to being frightened. But, things had changed rapidly, and the mess of his life became clearer as his breathing became more and more labored.

He felt as though he could not focus on his surroundings—as if he were in some other hazy atmosphere. His eyes gazed around his office at what used to be familiar. The art, the bookshelves—everything bled together like the colors of a cheap painting left in the rain. One wall was completely covered in books—encyclopedias, textbooks, journals, various novels written by colleagues. He had a special section on the second shelf for his own completed novels, fifteen in all.

He didn't feel his usual sense of pride here. How could he when he couldn't distinguish one object from another? Everything that had been important to him—everything he had worked his entire life for—didn't matter anymore.

A dark mahogany desk covered in scattered papers and unopened envelopes took up half the room. The papers on his desk never made it to the fireplace where he usually disposed of letters written by a large array of his readers. The roaring fire grew taller and fiercer as Vincent melted into the leather of his favorite chair.

Besides the crackling of the fire and the thoughts racing through his head, the only other sound Vincent heard was the soft whir of his computer. Rarely did he turn off his computer. Research was his life—up until recently. Every book he had written had been filled with facts from doctors, detectives, scientists, journals and any other specialists he required for his current project.

There would be no more projects for the great Vincent Kraver.

In a fit of panic, Vincent reached for the phone on the table next to his chair. Miscalculating its position, his hand sent the phone, along with a lamp, flying off the table and onto the floor. A thundering crash echoed in the enclosed space. The crash of the phone wasn't nearly as loud as the crash of Vincent's heart when his office door swung open and he stared into the eyes of his killer.

ONE

Ten days earlier

Vincent looked around the crowded room hoping to find interesting characters. These events were usually attended by unique people whom he could save for future projects. One man looked like he was about to fall over from exhaustion. He eyes were half closed (or half open, he couldn't really decide) and his body was leaning a little to the left. With his pale skin and distant gaze, Vincent calculated he had been standing in line without food or drink for at least two hours. Standing in line for hours can be tiring, but at least there was a good payoff. He gets to meet Vincent Kraver after all. And, maybe afterwords, he could audition for the part of zombie number 67 in *Night of the Dawn of the Dead.*

What could be better than meeting Vincent Kraver, author of fifteen bestselling novels? With any luck, in a few weeks that number would rise to sixteen. Vincent was positive the novel he had recently completed would join his previous ones on the best seller tables in bookstores. He'd found his niche in writing early in life. He used his talent to build a life for himself that he never would have imagined having when he was a child. After all he had been through to get to where he is today, the line out the door for his autograph was the least he could expect, even if most of the people waiting were slightly less intelligent than those Vincent would usually choose to converse with.

Another woman standing a few spots behind the zombie was thumbing through the pages of a book, reading bits and pieces and acting as though she were reading a letter from the Savior himself. Her eyes were glued to the novel. She was biting her nails and slightly bending and straightening her knees, simulating a pious individual deep in prayer. He could hear a little "amen" in her thoughts whenever she finished a paragraph.

The book she's holding could certainly be considered the Bible. It was written by a god.

The author smiled inwardly at his witty thought as he glanced at the book in front of him. It was opened to the title page: *Quiet Thunder* by Vincent Kraver. It was his latest novel, soon to be at the top of all booklists in prestigious magazines. The thought sent tingles up his spine. There was a post-it on the page with the name "Kenny" scrawled across it in his assistant's bubbly handwriting. Vincent glanced up at Kenny who had wide eyes and an even wider grin.

"It is such an honor to meet you, Mr. Kraver," he said, a slight tremble in his voice. "I've read all your books. So moving and inspiring."

"Really? You've read them all?" Vincent narrowed his eyes challengingly at Kenny. "What was your favorite?"

"Oh, God. Such a tough question." Kenny looked around as he pondered his answer. "I'd have to say *Fake Nails, False Lashes*. That was a real page-turner. I couldn't put it down."

"Thank you very much, Kenny."

"You take detective novels to a whole new level," Kenny continued.

Smiling politely at this compliment that he had heard numerous times over the past two hours, he quickly wrote, "Dear Kenny, God bless," and handed the novel back across the table. "The pleasure's all mine." As his fan walked away, Vincent considered how stale the name Kenny was. It would never work for a hero in any piece of fiction. No one would turn three hundred pages for a guy named Kenny—unless he had an intriguing last name.

Vincent looked down at his watch. He had been sitting here for two hours already, and from the length of the line, he would guess he had at least another hour or two of pointless chatter with his readers. If they weren't paying $25.95 a pop for his novels, he would not bother to show up to these signings. He was never a very social person, and small talk was not a skill at which he excelled. He much preferred the solitude of his office at home where he could write his thoughts down rather than verbalize them.

Without a glance at his next autograph-seeking fan, Vincent stood up and walked towards the restroom. He held up an empty water bottle for his agent to see, indicating the need for a break. The bathroom was thankfully empty. Vincent remembered his last book signing when a man approached him at the urinals and started up a conversation that he couldn't easily talk his way out of. That was a disaster which he hoped he would never have to endure again.

Turning on the faucet, Vincent made sure the water was freezing before splashing it on his face. His hand was already sore and he wasn't looking forward to signing his name for more people. Oh well. He knew what he had to do. After checking his appearance in the mirror (powerful, not large, he always told himself), Vincent exited the bathroom and made his way through the stacks to the signing table. He was glad to see his agent put another bottle of water by his seat.

Looking into the crowd, Vincent spotted his assistant, Sharla. She was walking up and down the aisles with her Post-its and Sharpie marker. He knew she would be repeating the same dialogue over and over again with each customer.

Name.

Mine?

Who would you like the book dedicated to?

Oh.

Please open to the title page.

Why?

So Mr. Kraver doesn't have to search for the page.

Oh.

Vincent knew Sharla hated book signings, but she repeated her conversation with a smile on her face. He certainly paid her enough.

"Oh my God! I've read all your books. *Red Carpet* was totally my favorite. I can't wait to read this one. What's your inspiration?" The girl holding the Bible was finally at the front of the line. Vincent looked at the post-it and pasted a smile on his face.

"Well, Genevieve, people like you are my inspiration."

"Wow," said Genevieve as she watched him write "God bless."

Vincent watched Genevieve as she walked away and wondered if she prayed every night in front of a cross with him on it. Other than the fact that Jesus had long hair and enemies, Vincent didn't think it was too much of a stretch.

"Goodbye, Genevieve," he whispered. Genevieve, now there's a name worth reading.

An hour and a half later, the last fan had finally left the book store. Vincent stood up from the table and stretched, slowly uncurling his pen-holding hand one finger at a time. Relieved to have gotten through another book signing, he waited impatiently as

Devon, his agent, shook hands with the store owner. When Devon looked over at him, Vincent gave a slight motion of his head toward the door indicating he would wait for him outside.

Vincent usually left the socializing to Devon. Hadn't he done enough of it already with all the customers?

The chilly November air felt good on his hot skin. It didn't matter how low any store set the thermostat – Vincent always felt like he had his own warm climate. He wiped sweat from his brow with his handkerchief and made a swipe over the rest of his balding head. The little hair that hung on was more of a white fuzz that Vincent refused to shave off. His wife encouraged him to embrace the aging process. Vincent, however, wasn't ready to let go of his youth, despite being in his mid-fifties.

He leaned against the side of the building letting the cool brick relieve the flushed skin of his neck. Pulling his cell phone out of his pocket, he checked the time: 7:43. He would have to call Lillian and tell her he would be late. He was expected home around 8:00 for the usual Sunday dinner with his family. Because the book signing was in Ridgewood, he wouldn't get home to Morristown till at least 8:30.

Sunday night was usually stressful for him and his family. Dinner was meant to bring the family closer together since their weekly schedules were so incompatible. For some reason, however, sitting and dining together seemed to create more distance between Vincent, his wife, and his two children. Vincent reminded himself that Neil and Susan were in high school, so the distance they put between themselves and their parents was typical. Sunday dinner always felt more like a painful obligation than a pleasant family bonding.

He was about to dial home when he heard the slow approach of footsteps. Vincent looked up expecting to see Devon walking towards him. Instead, he looked up at someone much more intriguing. A man dressed completely in black approached Vincent holding a copy of *Quiet Thunder* close to his chest. His long black hair hung unkempt over his dark eyes. The temperature seemed to drop as the man moved forward, yet somehow beads of sweat still formed along Vincent's receding hairline.

"I'm sorry but the signing is over," muttered Vincent as the dark character got closer.

"What makes you think I want your autograph?" the stranger replied harshly. The raspy voice sent a chill up Vincent's spine.

An awkward couple of seconds passed before Vincent responded. "Who are you?" he asked, more fascinated than nervous of this person's eeriness.

The man reached up and adjusted a pair of sunglasses that Vincent hadn't noticed. "I'm your biggest fan," he said with an evil grin. The sarcasm in his voice was palpable, and an uneasy energy was left in the air as he walked by. Vincent watched the man's back until he disappeared around a corner. His gaze was fixed in the direction the dark stranger retreated until...

"Hey, Vince. Ready to go?" Devon's voice snuck in.

"I was ready ten minutes ago."

"Well, one of us has to be social, and since you insist on being the elusive, standoffish writer, it has to be me."

"I'm not standoffish," Vincent retorted. "I'm mysterious."

Devon gave a smile which Vincent read as fake. "If you insist."

Vincent rode shotgun in Devon's beat up minivan. "Why are you still driving this piece of crap? Don't you get fifteen percent of my book earnings?"

"Yes," Devon answered. "I also have a wife, four kids, and a less extravagant standard of living than you."

Vincent leaned back and rubbed his hand, which was still sore from "blessing" so many of his books. "Thank God that's over. I thought my hand was gonna cramp up."

"Just think of it as a warm up for the next couple of months."

"Boston, Chicago, Denver, and...Seattle?"

"Yeah."

"Great," Vincent said in a tone that clearly wasn't excited.

Devon let out an exasperated sigh. "If you hate book signings so much, you should stop having them."

"I thought you said book signings were essential to a book becoming a bestseller," said Vincent.

"Most of the time. Depends on the author."

"Well, I think I'm established enough to not have to do these signings anymore." The rest of the drive was silent with the exception of stupid conversations on the radio that Vincent managed to block out. About forty-five minutes later, Vincent looked out his window as the van pulled up the driveway of an absurdly large house in the middle of Morristown. Morristown, New Jersey was becoming known for its "McMansions" as they added an out-of-place detail to the woodsy atmosphere.

"Thanks for the ride," said Vincent. "Hopefully my car will be ready tomorrow. You know how meticulous Mercedes mechanics are."

"Yeah," replied Devon. "'Cause I deal with Mercedes mechanics all the time." Vincent took note of the sarcasm in his agent's comment. He didn't like it. "Look, Vincent, if you don't want to be a famous author who attends book signings, stop writing books."

"How could I do that to my fans? I set the bar high. They expect great things from me."

"Then stop complaining. Go have dinner."

"Oh, hell." Vincent slammed the door as he realized he forgot to call Lillian to say he'd be late. He trudged up the steps to his four-story palace and braced himself for his wife's anger.

TWO

When Vincent walked into his house, the first thing he noticed was the blaring Metallica coming from upstairs. Neil, his son, rarely kept his music at an appropriate decibel. When they asked him to lower the volume, it would quiet down for about five minutes before slowly creeping up until it was louder than before. At seventeen years old, there was no way Neil would start obeying his parents now.

Vincent walked up the stairs and pounded on the door. "How's your essay going?"

"What?"

"Can you lower that?" Neil turned down the volume before his father continued. "Did you work on your essay?"

"No, I've been busy."

"Did you even start it?"

"No, but I have a pretty good idea."

"Don't you think it's time you got started? You don't have much time."

"Four months, Dad. That's more than enough time."

"Don't expect to get into Princeton, or any top school for that matter, without putting some serious thought into your essay."

"I know." Neil turned up his music to full volume more to annoy his father than for his own entertainment. Neither of them wanted to have this conversation about his college entry essay again. So, Vincent headed back downstairs hoping to find peace in his office.

He couldn't help but notice the smell of what he knew was Lillian's usual Sunday night feast emanating from the kitchen: chopped sirloin steak topped with mushrooms and onions, mashed potatoes, peas and carrots. He prided himself in marrying a renowned chef. Whenever Lillian decided to use her culinary skills in their own kitchen, it was sure to be a good night, at least for the taste buds. He tried to sneak past the kitchen without her noticing, but his wife managed to catch him with the eyes in the back of her head.

"How was the book signing?"

"Same."

"Long?"

"And, boring."

"It'll take me about ten minutes to warm up dinner." There was a definite edge to her voice as she tried to contain her anger.

"Sorry, I forgot to call," Vincent said. He hoped his apology didn't sound too forced. It wasn't something he gave to anyone very often. Lillian's silence was loud and clear, so Vincent continued to the safety of his office.

The tiny table outside his office door was piled high with mail. He didn't allow his mail to be brought into his office. He didn't allow anyone—not even his wife and kids—access to his office. He grabbed the pile and unlocked the door.

Vincent valued his privacy. His office was his sanctuary. It was very rare that anyone was invited in for any reason other than business, and even those meetings were kept as short as possible.

His face felt warm after the brief encounter with Neil and Lillian. He lowered the thermostat and sat down behind his desk to check his email. Many of them were from his readers praising him and asking for feedback on their own works. He deleted those emails without reading them. He went through the mail he found outside his office. The vast majority of it was fan mail. This was normal and he was quite used to being adored by his readers. He had a way with words, and it pleased him to know that others realized it as well.

The rest of the mail was junk and bills. He threw the junk in the shredder next to his desk and put the bills aside for his wife to go through later. Lillian always took care of the bills. It's true, Vincent Kraver had a way with words, but numbers were another story. He trusted Lillian more than himself to pay their bills. Besides, wasn't it usually the wife's job to spend her husband's money?

Vincent's cell phone started chirping. He looked at it. It was Lillian calling from the kitchen.

"Hello?"

"Dinner's ready."

"Okay, I'll be right in."

Lillian was hanging up the phone as Vincent walked into the kitchen, probably after calling Susan and Neil to let them know dinner was ready.

"Were you home all day?" Vincent asked.

"No, I went shopping with Franci. Why?"

"Neil needs someone here to force him to do his work. He's procrastinating way too much."

"He's not procrastinating," Lillian defended. "He's under a lot of pressure. It's enough that his teachers are getting on his case lately. He doesn't need it from you too."

"What are you talking about? I'm his father. I'm supposed to provide the pressure."

"No, you're supposed to ease the pressure. Not make it worse."

"Besides, what pressure does he have? If you ask me, he needs more pressure. He's spoiled. That's the problem."

Lillian shook her head. "No, that's not the problem. Imagine having a father as successful as you. Teachers expect amazing things from Vincent Kraver's son. It's a lot to deal with. He needs to work at his own pace."

"Well, unfortunately, I can't imagine having a successful father. Just a lunatic mother."

"You'd think you would treat your son with more love and support after your own father abandoned you," Lillian said as she plopped the food on the table.

"I'm trying my best. And there's no way Neil is going to amount to anything if he doesn't become a self-starter. That's how I earned my success."

Footsteps sounded in the hall. "Let's save this conversation for later," said Lillian as their children entered the kitchen. Neil had his earphones and iPod on until his mother gave him a pleading look to take them off. Susan, Vincent's fourteen-year-old daughter, plopped into her chair after adjusting her hip-hugger jeans. Everything she wore lately seemed to emphasize her growing curves, and her pants always looked like they were ready to burst at the seams. Vincent made no attempt to understand the fashion trends of today's youth.

The first few minutes of dinner were silence-filled with the exception of the clanking plates and utensils. Susan spooned herself a generous helping of mashed potatoes and put them next to her mountain of steak. Vincent squirmed in his seat as he watched his daughter cover everything in a river of gravy.

"Susan, maybe you should eat half of that and save the rest for lunch tomorrow."

Susan shot Vincent a shocked look.

"What are you saying?" she asked

"Well..." Vincent tried to choose his words carefully. "Well, if you look at me, you'll notice obesity runs in the family. Unfortunately, that means you're genetically inclined to be larger than some girls. But you can conquer that by watching what you eat."

"Vincent, that's enough," Lillian whispered harshly.

Susan's eyes welled up.

"I'm just trying to help. Can't I be concerned about my daughter's appearance?"

"Okay! Fine! Thanks for the advice," Susan jumped in. "Can we change the topic now?"

A few more moments of awkward silence passed before Lillian spoke. "So, have you decided who you want to ask to the winter ball yet, sweetie?" Vincent watched as Lillian tried to converse with their son. Talking to Neil was like talking to a brick.

"No," Neil replied. "The girls at my school are so shallow."

"That's not true," said Susan.

"You're only a freshman, dumbass. You haven't been there long enough to judge."

Lillian gave Neil a stern look. "Watch your language. We'll have none of that at the dinner table."

Neil rolled his eyes. "Fine, I'll tell her she's a dumbass after dinner."

"Neil!" This time it was Vincent's voice that cut off his son's. "Can we please have a nice family dinner for once?"

The rest of the "nice" dinner continued in silence. After returning to his office, Vincent sat back in his chair, relieved to have gotten through another evening with his wife and kids. They were fine to be around in small doses. But after hours of signing books for people who thought themselves to be intellectuals, he was just not in any mood for more socializing.

The calm didn't last very long, however, as the door flew open and Lillian burst in raging. Vincent silently scolded himself for forgetting to lock the door.

"What kind of father do you think you are, talking to Susan like that?"

Vincent was taken aback by the sudden intrusion. "I'm trying to be a concerned father who cares about his daughter's health. She's been gaining weight all through middle school. Don't tell me you haven't noticed."

"There's a difference between being concerned and being overly critical, Vincent. What you said was just mean."

"I was truthful."

Vincent's answer did nothing to allay his wife's anger. "You know what? I don't want to see you for the rest of the night. Sleep here, in your damn sanctuary!"

He winced when Lillian slammed the door behind her. Their fights were getting more frequent, and he knew they needed to find a balance between them in order to work things out. This was something he would never say out loud, however, because letting people know you were willing to give meant they'd walk all over you from then on. Vincent knew this, and he would never give in.

He turned to his work to take his mind off of his marital problems. The mail on his desk was a large assortment of sizes and colors. Most were regular white letter-sized envelopes, but Vincent got the occasional pink, blue, or green envelope with stickers and an address in perfect handwriting. If he was lucky, an occasional envelope was scented. Women always wanted to send little pieces of themselves. One woman actually sent him a handful of her eyelashes as a sign of her adoration. That woman must have been thrilled when the murderer in his next novel collected eyelashes from all of his victims.

Vincent flicked a small switch next to the fireplace and two seconds later, a fire roared to life. The busy author rarely had the time or energy to read his fan mail. He threw the letters one at a time into the flames until one caught his eye. An envelope covered in glitter and puff paint appeared halfway through the pile. He even noticed how the i's were dotted with stars. The return address said the letter came from a Miss Kimberly Philips of Pulaski, Tennessee. He felt bad ripping the Hello Kitty sticker used to seal the envelope.

Dearest Vincent,

I cannot even begin to tell you how much I enjoy reading your books. Your characters are bound by an emotional core that weaves them together into an intrinsic quilt of psychological and sobering reality.

Vincent paused as he tried to wrap his head around the idea of a "weaving core" and a "sobering quilt." He couldn't help but wonder if Kimberly even knew what the word "intrinsic" meant.

With every novel that I read, I find myself connecting to characters in ways I never thought possible. Whether it's Mrs. Peterson in Love Me Once, Kill Me Twice *or Ramone in* Graffiti Room, *I always find a little piece of myself that I never knew existed.*

A chuckle escaped Vincent's lips as he read that last sentence. I guess he should feel accomplished that he was able to help what he could only guess was a twelve-year-old girl find herself in a seventy-six-year-old comatose woman and a transsexual prostitute who killed his clients with a nail file.

Vincent could not understand how many of the people who called themselves "his" fans didn't seem like they could understand Mother Goose without a dictionary. To make his novels as realistic and accurate as possible, most of his time during the writing process was spent doing thorough research. Vincent had intended his work to appeal to intellectuals with a love of mystery and suspense, not little girls like Kimberly who clearly couldn't write a coherent letter.

He decided he could not read any more of Kimberly's letter without his IQ dropping fifteen points. He opened his desk drawer and filed it in a folder labeled "Character Concepts." Vincent always found his best character profiles in that folder.

He continued to sift through his fan mail. There were many big yellow envelopes stuffed to capacity. He knew these were manuscripts of wannabe authors looking for feedback. He usually just tossed these into the fire without looking at them. It's not like he had spare time to criticize other people's works, especially when he knew they probably wouldn't be any good. Vincent didn't like to waste his time. If people were smarter, they'd know how busy he was.

He tossed them one by one into the fireplace, and the pile of mail grew shorter and shorter as most of the manuscripts were hundreds of pages long. Just as he was getting to the bottom of the pile, one of the large envelopes caught his attention. Along with Vincent's address, there was a message scrawled along the bottom.

In your best interest...

That note, however, was not what caught his eye. What kept Vincent from throwing it in with the other manuscripts was the picture glued on the corner.

"Well, that's interesting," Vincent said feeling his pulse quicken. Staring back at him from the photo was a baby boy wearing a t-shirt covered in turtles. "Very interesting indeed." Vincent tore open the envelope that included his baby picture glued to the front, anxious about what he would find inside.

THREE

Kraver by Kevin Larre

Dramatic Beginnings

Janet Kraver lay on the table in the middle of the delivery room completely exposed. Nothing could have prepared her for what she just went through. She was always told bringing a baby into the world was a beautiful thing. It was natural and a part of life that every woman dreamed of doing someday. Well, whoever thought childbirth was beautiful was either blind or delirious. There was nothing beautiful about the ripping, the tearing, and the sheer torture she went through.

She had also been told of the magical feeling every mother felt when she heard her baby's first cries. Once again, however, Janet was left wanting. She didn't hear her baby. She didn't even see him. Where had they taken him? She wanted to hold her son. She'd just gone through hours of endless pain and felt she deserved to see the result of her labor.

She was wondering where they took her baby. She had pushed for hours. She knew he had come out. She felt the enormous pressure pass through her fragile body. Then, as the pain finally subsided, a wave of relief rippled through her. This was quickly replaced by anxiety and fear.

Where were her baby's screams? Didn't babies usually cry when they came out? She was so tired. All she wanted to do was hold her baby close and rest. Where was her baby? Why wasn't he crying? She reached her hand out to a nurse rushing by. Before she could say anything, the nurse reassured her they were doing all they could.

What did she mean? What was wrong? She started to yell. She screamed for her baby. She yelled that they were kidnapping him. The doctors were criminals. They kidnapped her son. She screamed for help hoping someone would rescue her baby from the monsters who stole him. She kept on screaming. Voices tried to calm her down, but her anxiety increased with every moment that her child wasn't placed in her arms. Her arms and legs flailed about madly.

"Give me my baby! Give me my baby!"

Hands came down on her in an attempt to control her thrashing body. Her rage could not be diminished.

"I want my baby! Give me my baby! GIVE ME MY BABY!"

She barely felt the prick of the needle in her arm. She was still screaming when everything around her began to swirl. The lights grew very bright before everything completely disappeared in blackness.

It was in this manner that Vincent Kraver was welcomed into the world.

The hospital room had no decorations. There were no flowers, no balloons—not even a card to congratulate the sleeping woman who had just given birth to her first child. Nurses gathered in groups when the excitement of the maternity ward occasionally subsided. They talked about the poor woman in room 207 who had no visitors. Didn't she have any family? A friend? New mothers were normally swarmed by family members and friends who were dying to soak up the sights and sounds of the new babies. Janet Kraver—such a poor woman—had no one.

Janet woke up in the hospital bed in her private room. She barely remembered what had happened only a few hours earlier. With anxiety still lingering, she looked around the room. It was then she remembered and her anxiety grew. Where was her baby?

"Excuse me?" she called, hoping a nurse or doctor could hear her through her closed door. "Hello?" No response.

Her head fell back against the pillow as she exhaled deeply. She tried to remember the breathing exercises her therapist had taught her when in a stressful situation. Looking

around her, she found the call button to alert the nurse's station. She grabbed it and pressed as hard as she could as if the harder she pushed, the faster someone would come. She pressed the button eleven times before the door to her room finally opened.

A nurse came in followed by the doctor. "Good morning, Ms. Kraver," the nurse said politely. "How are you feeling?"

"Where's my son?"

"Ms. Kraver."

"Where's Vincent?"

"Ms. Kraver!" The doctor's voice was sharp. The nurse flinched at his startling tone. "Vincent is fine," he continued, this time making his voice softer, more comforting. "Please calm yourself."

Janet took a few deep breaths before speaking again. There was still a shakiness in her voice that she couldn't control. "Please...please tell me where my son is."

"He's in the nursery."

"Why haven't I seen him?"

"There were complications."

Janet ignored the nurse as she walked around her bed checking the various tubes and beeping machinery. "What do you mean?"

"You were in active labor for nearly ten hours. In most cases, we would have recommended a c-section, but since that wasn't your birth plan we proceeded with a natural birth. Of course, if you hadn't remained conscious, we would have had no choice."

"I didn't want a c-section," Janet interrupted.

"I know, and you didn't end up needing one. You were able to remain strong."

Janet ignored the compliment. "So, then what happened? What complications were there?"

"Vincent was in a difficult position. His body was slanted, making him come out a bit sideways." The nurse let out a little moan at the thought of such torture. "To make matters more complicated," the doctor continued, "the umbilical cord was wrapped around his neck twice. This cut off oxygen circulation to the brain. In order to get him out, we had to go in with forceps and pull him out."

"Forceps!"

"There were no other options. He would have suffocated." The doctor's voice remained calm in order to not further excite the frightened mother.

"But he's okay? You said he's in the nursery, didn't you?"

"Yes. We had to give him CPR. He wasn't breathing. But, everything is fine. His vitals are normal. As far as we can tell, there is no permanent damage."

"Is there any temporary damage?"

"There are some marks on his scalp from the forceps. Battle wounds I guess you could call them," he said smiling in an attempt to dull her apprehension. "They shouldn't last. He's going to be just fine."

Janet smiled for the first time since the delivery. The nurse looked at her. "Is there anything I can get you, Ms. Kraver?"

"Can I please see my son now?"

"Of course."

A few minutes later, Janet Kraver was holding Vincent Kraver: eight pounds, two ounces, twenty-one inches. Two red scabs remained on either side of his bald head where the forceps had grabbed him. Vincent began to whimper as he awoke from his nap. Janet's eyes filled with tears as Vincent finally made the sounds she had longed to hear in the delivery room.

Janet walked home from the hospital with Vincent in a rickety stroller. Her purple backpack had extra clothes, money, and identification. She also managed to hold onto three plastic bags full of bottles, diapers, baby wipes, baby shampoo, triscuits, and milk. She walked despite the fact that the hospital was fifty-three blocks from her apartment. She had splurged on a cab to get to the hospital when she went into labor and didn't have enough for a ride back.

Things had been tight since Arnie left her. Janet no longer had anyone to take care of her. She no longer felt the security that she felt when her boyfriend was around. She really thought he was the one. They had been together for nearly ten months when he walked out on her and his unborn child. Janet was able to get a job at the supermarket down the street where Arnie was the manager. She moved into his apartment a week after meeting him. Everything finally seemed perfect. That is, until Janet found out she was pregnant. She knew instantly that Arnie didn't want the baby. He had told her on more than one occasion to have it "taken care of." Janet would respond by calling him a criminal and a murderer. It's true, the fights were getting more frequent, but what was a relationship without fights?

At least he left and didn't kick her out. Most guys packed up her bags for her and put them in the hallway, leaving her to the streets until she found someone new to love

and move in with. Arnie had been nice enough to leave some cash and a note that said, "I can't. I'm sorry." It hurt, but Janet learned long ago to get used to disappointment.

Janet looked down at Vincent's innocent, chubby face. She thought about what a hassle it would be raising him on her own. How could she care for him when there was no one to care for her?

"When you're older, you'll be able to take care of your mommy, right?" Vincent responded by spitting up on the blanket Janet had stolen from the hospital. Janet reached into her coat pocket and found a crumpled up tissue. She folded it over until she found an unused section and wiped the white liquid dripping from her son's pursed lips.

Janet and Vincent finally reached the entrance to their building. Janet surveyed all she had to carry up the stairs. She wished now, more than ever, that the building had an elevator. How was she supposed to carry the groceries and the stroller with the baby up the stairs? She decided that two trips were in order.

"Okay, Vincent," she said. "I'll be right back. Mommy just needs to drop this stuff off. You behave yourself." Janet moved the stroller off to the side of the entryway before struggling up the stairs with the grocery bags. She got to her door before realizing she left the key to her apartment in the

cup holder of the stroller. She put her load down and went back down the stairs.

"Oh my God! Vincent?" Janet nearly fainted when she came out of the stairwell and found Vincent was gone. She ran out the door and onto the sidewalk screaming Vincent's name. She looked down the street and was relieved to see her son had not gotten very far. A little girl, probably around seven years old, was pushing Vincent's stroller, skipping, and humming to herself.

"Hey, girlie! Stop right there!" shouted Janet. The mini-kidnapper stopped short and spun around causing her blonde braids to whip against her freckled face. Janet ran up to her with flames in her eyes. "What the hell do you think you're doing? You can't just go around stealing people's babies!"

"I didn't steal him. He wasn't with anyone." The girl's green eyes stared defiantly up at Janet.

"Excuse me? This boy is mine! This is my baby!"

"Finders keepers, losers…"

Janet smacked the girl as hard as she could before grabbing the handles of the stroller and heading back towards her apartment. Without looking back, Janet could hear the little girl's sniffles and her footsteps as she ran away.

Janet sat at her kitchen table wondering when the screaming would stop. She did all she could think of to ease whatever pain Vincent was in, but his cries persisted. Dropping her pencil, she marched over to the stroller in the corner of the room and knelt down so she was eye to eye with Vincent.

"What? What do you want?" Janet ripped off her shirt revealing her swollen breasts. She hated breast feeding and didn't bother wearing a bra anymore. Her breasts were way too sore to be contained so tightly. "Are you hungry? Is this what you want?" she asked pointing to her chest.

Janet lifted Vincent from the stroller and pressed him close to her nipple. He made no attempt to latch on, leaving Janet more frustrated. She hated not knowing what was wrong with her baby. She wondered when he would start talking. It would make her life so much easier if he could just tell her what was bothering him.

Walking back over to the table, Janet placed Vincent down to check on his diaper. After looking, she found nothing solid in it. She didn't give him a new diaper unless he did a number two. He may have been wet, but because of the expense of diapers, Janet had to do everything she could to cut back on costs, which meant leaving Vincent in diapers until they were utterly soiled.

Janet put Vincent back in his stroller and rolled him over to the table so she could continue her work. Vincent's screams continued without any intermission. At this point, there was really nothing more Janet could do. Her son would just have to learn to be stronger and cope with the fact that life wasn't perfect.

The blank piece of paper on the kitchen table stared up at Janet waiting to be made into a work of art. Janet had always felt she had the potential to become an amazing artist, and now that she had a child, she felt it was her responsibility to use her talent to be lucrative. She had never seriously pursued her art dream before because she was usually held back by unambitious boyfriends and dead-end jobs that took up most of her time.

She thought being with Arnie would free up her time and give her more freedom to explore her artistic capabilities. He was, after all, the manager of the supermarket where she worked. He was in charge of schedules, and she hoped he would favor her and nurture her desires. Instead, Arnie took full advantage of her, making her work insanely long hours and forcing her to come in to cover for anyone who called in sick. Since she lived with him, she could never lie and call in sick. She could barely lie well over the phone, let alone in person.

"Would you shut up!" she yelled at her screaming baby. "Mommy has to work!" Not surprisingly, Vincent continued screaming even louder than before. Janet couldn't take it anymore. She grabbed her keys and stormed out of the apartment, leaving Vincent to cry on his own.

When she returned an hour later, Vincent was sleeping. Janet once again took a seat at the table and got to work.

The streets were crowded with the usual bustle of pedestrians heading to their jobs. Janet's table was lined with her various pieces of artwork. She was sure they would make her some money and get her artistic career off the ground.

The large array of pictures made Janet very proud. She thought she finally found her calling that would support her and Vincent. Looking over to the end of her display table, Janet saw her son bundled up in blankets in his stroller. He looked around at everything with bright, inquisitive eyes. He hardly cried anymore, and Janet was sure the weeks of having his cries ignored finally took the urge to complain out of him.

"What is this supposed to be?" asked a random passerby.

"Well, hello," said Janet with the voice of someone ready to make her first sale. "As you can see, I can create any

kind of picture, but I specialize in drawing animals. This fellow here is a turtle."

"Really?" said the customer. "I thought it was a ladybug."

Janet studied the drawing closely before responding. "It certainly could be a ladybug."

The customer looked confused. "Well, which is it? A turtle or a ladybug?"

"It's whatever you want it to be. That's the beauty of my artwork. You can interpret it in many different ways."

"How much are you charging for your work?"

"Fifteen dollars apiece."

"Fifteen dollars? What a rip off. My seven-year-old daughter has more realistic doodles in her school notebook."

"Well if that's how you feel about my work, maybe you should just leave." The customer rolled his eyes before walking away. "Don't ever let people tell you your work is no good," Janet said to Vincent. "You'll never get anywhere if you don't try."

"That's good advice," said a male voice. Janet turned around and was blown away by the extraordinarily good looking man smiling at her.

"Thank you," Janet replied. "I'm glad someone thinks so."

"I wish my parents were supportive of my career path. I'm a photographer, but of course they wanted me to be a doctor or a lawyer."

"My parents weren't supportive of me either. I ran away when I was fourteen, and I've never regretted it."

Janet and the man, Dmitri, ended up talking for hours, and Janet sold none of her artwork. Feeling bad for having distracted her from conducting any business, Dmitri bought every piece Janet had displayed. Janet fell in love immediately and invited Dmitri to live with her and Vincent.

One week later, Dmitri moved in.

Three months later, Janet found her and Vincent's things in the hall, along with the artwork Dmitri had bought. The locks had been changed. Janet and Vincent were homeless.

FOUR

Vincent stared dumbly at the pages, not knowing what to think after reading about the first few months of his life. He looked at the name of the author—Kevin Larre. Kevin Larre? Vincent didn't know anyone named Kevin Larre. He had met many people in his life and wasn't always the best at remembering names. However, with all the details Kevin Larre was able to provide in his brief manuscript about Vincent's very early childhood, this writer must be a person whom Vincent has been in close contact with for a very long time. The more he thought about it, the more convinced Vincent became that he had never heard of a man named Kevin Larre.

Whoever this guy was, he had clearly taken an interest in a worthwhile topic. Vincent's life had been dramatic since the day he was born, at least according to his mother. It was never safe to believe every word that came out of Janet Kraver's mouth. The stories she told of herself made her sound like a woman who attempted every possible dream one can have in life, and, therefore, had achieved so much more than the average person.

Vincent was aware that only half of that was true. His mother *did* go after her dreams. Every…single…one. The problem with Janet was she never finished anything she started. She went after her dreams but never saw them through. And she had so many dreams. Practically every month Janet Kraver announced a new goal in her life. In April, she wanted to be a gymnast. In May, she'd make plans to start her own newspaper. In June, she'd take a stab at being a wedding planner. Each month was something new to start and eventually leave unfinished.

Vincent was convinced his mother had some form of Attention Deficit Disorder. How could anyone who didn't suffer from ADD jump from one life purpose to another every thirty days? He was always afraid of turning into his mother and never settling on a direct path in life. So, when Vincent decided he was an extremely talented writer, he made sure to stick to that talent.

And, look where he was now. He had a career, money, family, fame, and not an ounce of his mother's personality to get in his way.

It was understandable that Janet Kraver never had the ability to keep a man in her life for more than a few months. Her personality was so unpredictable, it surprised him that his father had managed to stay with her for ten months. That must have been ten months of torture, especially when she was pregnant. If Vincent hadn't been biologically connected to Janet Kraver, he is sure he would have followed in the footsteps of all the other men.

Vincent walked over to his desk and put the Kevin Larre manuscript in the top drawer. He thought it was well written, and the subject matter was certainly attention-grabbing. However, the events of the day left him tired and unwilling to try and find out who the mystery author was. He went to the large wooden wardrobe and pulled out sheets and pillows. The act of making up the pullout couch in his office was becoming an unpleasant routine for him. Maybe tomorrow, he could bring up the mystery of Kevin Larre with Lillian and bury the fight from today.

It was eight-thirty when Vincent walked into the kitchen with an aching back. That damn pullout had a mountain in the middle that would throw Superman's back out of whack, though he probably should have been used to it by now given his and Lillian's recent history. They seemed to be getting into fights every other night now. He also knew, however, that Lillian had a very quick rebound rate and would be apologizing for not letting him in the bedroom. He, at least, hoped she would feel sorry since her way of apologizing usually involved delicious food. And, Vincent had woken up with a hefty appetite.

To his disappointment, Vincent walked into the kitchen and found Lillian sitting at the table with a bowl of oatmeal, a steaming cup of coffee, and a *Better Homes* magazine. There would normally be a healthy array of waffles, eggs, toasts, and bacon the night after they had a fight. He could tell she was still a little angry and decided not to mention Kevin Larre or the manuscript.

Vincent sighed audibly as he walked over to the coffee pot to pour himself a cup. He opened the refrigerator and searched for his low-fat lactose-free milk.

"Lil, where's my milk?"

"There's none in there?" she responded without looking up.

"I wouldn't be asking you if there was."

"If there's none in there then you probably finished it."

"But, why isn't there another carton? You usually get more when we're almost out."

Lillian looked up from her magazine. The look in her eyes told Vincent she didn't want to be having an argument with him this early in the morning. "You're the only one in this house that drinks that kind of milk. You need to tell me when it's low or else I won't know to buy more." With that, she looked back down at her magazine.

Vincent walked over to the table with a cup of black coffee. He winced as he took a sip. Lillian either didn't notice or didn't care.

"What are you doing today?" he asked her trying to sound amicable. If she was going to ignore being angry, so was he.

"I'm leaving in an hour to see my mother. She insists on getting a new cat even though Sugar just died a week ago."

"She did?"

"Yeah. I told you when it happened."

"Right, I forgot." This was a lie. Of course he remembered Lillian telling him the cat died. He was happy at the news. He hated cats.

"I don't understand it. Ever since my dad died, she's insisted on having a cat around to keep her company. I try to be there for her, but I get so tied down at the restaurant."

"If you don't want your mother to have a cat, just don't take her out to get one. Make her go out herself. She's not dead yet." Vincent saw his wife's body stiffen, and he actually felt bad for what he just said.

"Just because you treat your mother like she's a rat carrying the plague doesn't mean no one else in the world is caring. My mother is troubled and can't cope with her emotions about my father dying. I'm going to help her any way I can because I want to. Not because I have to."

"I don't treat my mother like a rat," said Vincent. "She also happens to be troubled. And, she's always been that way. I finally have enough money to get her help, and this makes me uncaring?"

"You basically put her away and then severed all contact with her."

"It's better for everyone that way. You wouldn't understand. You didn't grow up with her."

Vincent truly felt that he was helping his mother by placing her in assisted living. She had spent her whole life moving to different apartments, usually at the expense of whatever man she had temporarily wrapped around her finger. Now, because of Vincent's generosity, Janet Kraver would be able to live out the rest of her life in one environment. In his eyes, that made him a great son, and he wouldn't let anyone try to convince him otherwise.

Lillian looked back down at *Better Homes* and flipped through several pages. Vincent thought he had finally won the argument when his wife spoke again. "God help us if our children ever treat us that way."

Vincent stood up and walked to the sink. "I need more milk," he said as he dumped his black coffee down the drain. He walked out before giving Lillian another chance to speak.

Vincent staggered into his office feeling deflated after yet another argument with Lillian. He was disappointed that he couldn't bring up the manuscript he had received. It was an issue that he thought a husband should make his wife aware of, but after her neglect of his needs this morning, he didn't feel he had to let her in on his secret.

Not that he had much to say about the secret. He had never heard of Kevin Larre. He must be a new writer, but obviously already talented. Vincent was concerned, however, as to how Kevin knew such intimate details of his early childhood. He considered calling the police, but after writing so many crime novels, he knew he couldn't file a report on someone unless that person made a direct threat toward him. Kevin Larre had done no such thing.

The details in his writing were accurate—quite accurate in fact. How did he know about the scars from the forceps? Information about his life was out there for the public. He expected part of his personal life to seep into the masses due to the voluminous praises his books had received.

He hadn't ever talked about his scars though. The only way someone would know about them is by seeing them. They were visible when his hair was cut short. Then, the two bald spots on either side of his head were noticeable. Even then, however, only an extremely astute person with keen observational skills would have detected them.

Vincent decided that Kevin Larre was surely both astute and observant. He was also clearly interested in writing about fascinating topics. His life was certainly one that people would love to read about.

He picked up the envelope that the manuscript had come in. The baby picture in the corner was taken from the web site Devon had set up for him. Despite being jealous of his success, Vincent found Devon to be a great agent, going above and beyond what typical agents do for their clients. The web site he made for Vincent was in response to the overwhelming success of his first novel, *Pocket Lies*. The site kept his fans satisfied and Vincent's popularity soaring.

"Okay, Kevin, who the hell are you?"

With a shake of his mouse, his screensaver dissipated and the Google homepage showed up. After typing "Kevin Larre," the site showed there were zero hits on the name. Instead, he was asked if he meant Kevin Lare.

Vincent sat back in his chair and folded his hands above his head. If he hadn't been balding, he would have been curling his fingers in his hair and tugging. This was a nervous habit he'd had his entire life, and probably the reason he lacked hair now. After a few seconds, he reached for his phone to try another tactic.

Devon answered after the third ring.

"Have you ever heard of a writer named Kevin Larre?"

"Kevin Larre? Can't say I have," said Devon.

Vincent was disappointed that his agent wasn't familiar with him. He usually knew everyone in the business. "Well, he sent me a manuscript. Actually, just one section of a manuscript. It's pretty interesting."

"What's it about?"

“Me.”

“Oh, well, then of course you find it interesting.”

“It’s good though.”

“Good enough to get published?”

“I’m not sure yet. I need to read more.”

“Did you request more?”

“He didn’t leave any contact information. That’s why I called you.”

“Sorry, but I’ve never heard of him. I can call around and see if anyone else has. Can you send me the manuscript?”

Vincent swiveled in his chair, mulling over whether or not he wanted to give the manuscript to anyone.

“Vincent?” Devon broke the brief silence.

“Yeah, I’m still here. I think I’m gonna hang onto the manuscript. Just see if anyone else has heard of this guy.”

“Alright. Will do. Kevin Larre you said?” asked Devon.

“Yeah. L-A-R-R-E.”

“Okay, and don’t forget you have another book signing in a few days.”

“Thanks for ruining my day,” Vincent responded before hanging up.

Vincent ended the call before Devon could respond. He had been given no further information regarding the mysterious Kevin Larre. He was frustrated, and for the first time in his life, he was stumped. And, for some reason, he was satisfied.

FIVE

The next night, Vincent was out to dinner with Patrick Donway. "So, how's the family?"

Vincent took another swallow of his black Russian before answering. His friend was fittingly dressed for a psychologist—black suit pants, merlot colored, button-down shirt, and a black sports jacket. Patrick was obviously doing well for himself. Vincent only hoped he could say the same about his patients.

"How are they ever?" was Vincent's terse response.

"Come on, Vince, this is the first time in two weeks we're having dinner together. You can at least give me a response that's longer than four words and doesn't end in a question mark."

As much as Vincent hated to admit it, Patrick was right about how often they'd been able to see each other. He needed to try and make more time for his friend—for his only friend, not that he would ever say this out loud.

Vincent met Patrick thirty-five years ago at Morris High School. Patrick had been the new kid during his junior year. His parents' jobs transferred them to New Jersey. Unfortunately, that meant uprooting their entire lives from Patrick's childhood home in California. Eileen Donway, Patrick's younger sister, had no problems with the move. She was only in fourth grade and, unlike Patrick, extremely outgoing. She came home from her first day at Morris Elementary with twenty new best friends and an extremely busy weekend ahead of her.

Patrick's adjustment to life on the east coast was virtually nonexistent. He missed the friends that he grew up with on his street. He missed the seventy-degree weather in the middle of January. He was angry at his parents for changing their lives, and he was irritated at Eileen's happy acceptance of their coastal shift. He rarely went home after school in order to avoid starting the same continuous fight with his parents. Instead, Patrick found solace in his school's library. It was the only place for him where conversation wasn't an issue. The librarian was seventy-three years old and had the ears of a coyote. Anything above a whisper made her ears perk, and whoever was speaking got a severe chastisement and a lecture on the rules of the library.

It was here that Patrick Donway had met Vincent Kraver. He had noticed Vincent on his first day in the library sitting alone at a table in the corner and scribbling profusely in a ratty notebook. He was surrounded by stacks of books, most of them looking like scientific journals. Having a strong interest in science and medicine made Patrick want to walk up to Vincent and question him about whatever it was he was working on. However, anyone within twenty feet of Vincent could feel his vibes warding off anyone who might have wanted to approach. Combined with

Patrick's own sense of isolation, this remained the relationship status between him and Vincent for the next few months.

It wasn't until mid-January that Patrick was forced to make his first friend at Morris High. The final bell rang. As usual, he made his way to the library to do his homework and putter around until he decided to drag himself home. He entered the library, and he saw Vincent at his table in the corner. Unfortunately, every other table was taken up by students who were working on class projects together. Books were being passed around the tables with everyone trying to find another piece of useless information to include in their oral presentations.

Patrick was about to turn around and walk out when he glanced over at Vincent. He couldn't quite tell, but it seemed as though Vincent had been watching Patrick survey the room and quickly averted his eyes when he glanced over. Patrick decided to finally give it a shot and timidly walked over to Vincent's table.

"Hi…um…" Patrick rolled his eyes as he stuttered.

Vincent peered up from his work and looked Patrick up and down. "I don't have any kind of infectious disease or anything."

Patrick felt like an idiot and began to sway. "Right. I was just wondering, if, I could, if, um…"

Vincent watched Patrick as he stumbled over his words. After a few seconds, he couldn't take it anymore and cut him off. "Yes. You. Can. Sit. Here. If. You. Like." Patrick felt his face get hot and wanted to get out of the library. However, that would have meant dealing with his parents whom he still hadn't forgiven.

Patrick finally sat down. "Sorry. I don't mean to come off so dense. I'm just kind of having trouble adjusting. I'm the new kid, you know?"

"You were the new kid four months ago." Vincent returned his attention to his work.

"Well, yeah, but this isn't the most welcoming school. Most of the people here already have their friendship circles sealed."

"You don't seem to try very hard."

"Excuse me, but you don't seem to have many friends. How long have you been here?"

"Two years and counting."

"So, what's your excuse?"

Vincent put his pen down and looked around. His exhale told Patrick that he was not used to having a conversation other than being forced to speak in class. "I make it a point not to get too close with people." With that, Vincent picked up his pen again and continued to write.

Patrick wasn't happy to end the conversation at that. Vincent had piqued his interest, and it actually felt nice to talk to someone other than his parents and sister. This was probably because the talks with his family were more argumentative than conversational. "Are you gonna explain why you can't get close to people or do you want to remain mysterious and elusive?"

"I'd prefer mysterious and elusive, but you don't seem like the kind of person who would settle for that."

"It just seems like we could both use a friend. Might as well give some conversation a try."

Vincent drew in another annoyed breath before speaking. "Okay. Well, I grew up with my mother and no father. My father left my mother before I was born. Not that I blame him. My mother is a complete nutcase. It's a wonder I turned out the way I did instead of some raging lunatic."

After Vincent's initial comments about his mother, Patrick wondered if he'd picked the right person to start a potential friendship with. Vincent sounded like he was full of pent up anger. Of course, Patrick wasn't really one to talk since he avoided his family as much as possible.

"My mother could never settle on a lifestyle," Vincent continued. "One day, she wanted to own her own flower shop, but that went to hell when she realized she knew nothing about gardening or plants. She then had the dream of being a professional tap dancer. She moved onto another dream once she realized how expensive tap shoes are."

Patrick listened to Vincent's description of his mother with confusion. "That still doesn't explain why you don't like being close with anyone."

"Well, with my mother constantly changing her life dream, she was also constantly changing our address. Actually, most times our address changed because the guy she was with came to his senses and threw her out. We were never in the same place for more than six months. After the fifth move, I decided to hell with friends. Never any time or point to putting effort into relationships."

"That's kind of depressing."

"Kind of?" Vincent started to get more animated as he continued. "This is the first time we've ever stayed in one place for more than a year. Two years is like a lifetime."

"What's your mom doing now?" Patrick asked, hoping to hear about some kind of light at the end of the tunnel.

"She's a waitress. She takes a bus into the city looking for acting jobs. Her dream now is to be an actress."

"At least, she has a job now."

"Yeah, but she doesn't tell anyone that she's a waitress."

"I don't understand. What does she tell people?"

"She says she's an actress. I tell her that she isn't an actress if she hasn't acted in anything. But, she just says that being a waitress is part of being an actress. There's no other way to break into the business than to wait tables."

"So, being a waitress is the same thing as being an actress?"

"I guess so, according to my lunatic mother."

Patrick wondered about his next question and decided they were already deep enough in Vincent's history to ask. "I don't mean to sound too intrusive, but if your mother can't hold down a job for more than a few months at a time, how can she afford to send you to school here? I mean, Morristown is pretty expensive."

"That's a good point," Vincent replied. "It's actually kind of a funny story. My mom was hit by a cab."

Vincent enjoyed the confusion on Patrick's face. "She was hit by a cab? How is that funny?"

"Well, I guess it isn't what you'd label as 'haha' funny. We spent many years living in New York City, and, one day, about three years ago, my mom stepped off the curb and was hit by a cab. She wasn't badly hurt or anything. It was stopping to pick up some people and it tapped her. I actually wouldn't be surprised if she was the one who bumped into the cab. Anyway, she fell to the ground, acted all dramatic, told the courts that her injuries would prevent her from working to support her son. After all that, she ended up getting twenty thousand dollars."

"You don't think she was really hurt?" Patrick asked.

"It's highly unlikely. Every time she went to court, she was limping on a different leg."

Patrick laughed, finally seeing the humor in the situation.

"So, combine that money with the tips she's able to earn as a waitress, and here I am."

"But, she's not a waitress," Patrick pointed out.

"Right, right," Vincent corrected himself. "She's an actress."

"I guess your mom does sound a little quirky."

"Which is why I strive to be like my father."

"But, your father left your mother."

"Exactly." Vincent went back to writing in his notebook bringing the conversation to a close. Patrick delved into his backpack in search of his homework assignments. He couldn't focus on anything though, not after having finally made a new friend—especially one as interesting and profound as Vincent Kraver.

Patrick's voice jolted Vincent back to the present. "Don't make me psychoanalyze you, Vincent. I know how much you hate that, but I'll do it if it's the only way to have a conversation with you."

"Fine, fine," said Vincent with an exaggerated sigh. "Where should I start?"

"How about with Lillian?" suggested Patrick.

"Okay, Lillian. Well, she's still my wife, still a chef, and still the mother of my children."

"I figured as much. How's she doing?"

"She's doing fine for herself I guess. We've been having many arguments lately, though."

"About what?"

"She's getting a bit lazy when it comes to taking care of our home. There's never any good food in the house, including the milk that I need to drink. She says she's been stressed out about work, but she's a chef. What could she possibly be stressed about?"

"Well," said Patrick, "she's the *head* chef. Maybe, she needs to come up with new recipes. Or, maybe she's having trouble with another chef or a waiter."

"That shouldn't distract her from taking care of the family though."

"Maybe you should talk to her about it. Nicely."

"Believe me, I've tried." Vincent's voice started to get a little defensive. "Our talks just turn into arguments."

Sensing the agitation in his friend's voice, Patrick decided to shift the topic over to Vincent's kids. "What about Susan and Neil?"

"Unfortunately, Susan was the subject of one of our fights." Vincent paused when the waitress placed their entrees in front of them. Pat preferred his steak rare, and it looked like it was freshly slaughtered in the kitchen for him. He always made it clear that he liked his beef "still mooing" on the plate.

Vincent continued after the waitress walked away. "Susan's been gaining weight lately. When I brought it up to Lillian, she flipped out."

"How did you bring it up to her?"

"I told Susan during dinner that she should watch how much she eats because she has bad genes."

Patrick looked at Vincent dumbfounded. "I can see why Lillian flipped out. That's kind of harsh."

"You always say it's important to be straightforward and honest."

"True, but it's also important to use a little tact."

"There's not always room for tact." Vincent gulped the rest of his drink and signaled to the waitress for another one.

Patrick continued questioning Vincent. "Is Neil enjoying his senior year?"

"I'm not really sure," said Vincent. "He spends most of his time in his room with his music blaring. He rarely hears me knock when I go to talk to him. I just hope he's focusing on his college applications."

"Where's he applying?"

"Princeton, Yale, Dartmouth, Cornell. Ivy league."

"Wow! That's great."

"Yeah. The only problem is he got a 1250 on his SATs. Which is okay, but you need to be more than okay to get into Princeton."

"He'll need a killer essay," Patrick interrupted.

"That's what I told him. Hopefully, he'll realize that himself."

"Don't worry. I'm sure he'll do fine."

"I hope so. I'd hate to be the only success story in my family." The waitress came back over and placed a black Russian in front of Vincent. The drink barely touched the table before Vincent swiped it up and brought it to his lips.

Patrick decided to humor his friend. He raised his glass of wine which matched his shirt. "To Kraver success." Vincent stopped sipping his drink long enough to raise it to Patrick's glass before taking another swig. "Speaking of Kraver success," Patrick continued, "I read *Quiet Thunder,* another winner."

"Thanks." Vincent told Patrick about the horrible book signing he had to sit through. He repeated what he could remember of the letter from Kimberly of Pulaski, Tennessee.

"It sounds like you make quite an impression on people whether you want to or not," said Patrick with a hint of laughter.

"I don't know what it is. The books I write are meant for intelligent people. People who can appreciate how much effort I put into every word I put down on paper. I feel so under-appreciated."

"Excuse me while I stick my finger in my mouth," Patrick said.

Vincent asked, "What is that supposed to mean?"

"I mean," replied Patrick, "that you're sitting there complaining about having so many fans and so much mail from them, and then you grumble about being under-appreciated. It makes no sense."

"Well, it would be nice if some of my fan mail was from people who were up to my level of thinking."

"You know, you should really see a therapist to deal with your narcissism."

"I don't need a therapist. There's nothing wrong with *me*."

"That's exactly what a narcissistic person would say."

"If you're suggesting I start paying you for our talks, you are way off base."

"I have enough patients to fill my appointment book, thank you very much."

"Anyone interesting?"

"Not particularly. Why? Are you already doing research for another book?"

"Nope, no definite ideas. Just trying to spark some inspiration." Vincent considered telling Patrick of the manuscript he received from Kevin Larre. He decided against it.

"Well," said Patrick, "I'll keep my ears open for you."

Vincent laughed. "Maybe you should keep your ears open for your patients."

"Thanks for the tip," Patrick said as he soaked up sauce with a piece of his partly cooked cow.

Disgusting, Vincent thought.

The drive home from the restaurant gave Vincent time to think things through about Lillian, his kids and the unknown Kevin Larre. Unfortunately, it seemed the latter was what took up most of his attention.

He pulled into his garage and took his time turning off the engine. He was in no rush to enter his house. He knew Lillian was still angry at him, and he had no idea what to do to get back on her good side.

Vincent removed the key from the ignition and stared down at the other keys on the chain. There were seven keys all together. Each key was unique in size, color, shape, and wear. The key to his office exhibited the most fade and scrapes. Vincent did all his work in his office. Therefore, it was no surprise that the key to his office was the dullest of the set. The label at the top indicating what room it was for had faded over time from the pads of his thumb and index finger, not that he really needed a label on it. It was the only silver key with a jagged circular edge. There was one spare key to his office, and Vincent was the only person who knew its hiding place.

He started thumbing a key that wasn't nearly as worn as the key to his office. With its golden gleam, one could see that it was rarely used, and for a good reason. This key protected his most valued possession from the outside world. Its twin shared the same hiding spot as the spare key to his office. It was the key to the bottom drawer of his desk that housed old spiral notebooks of varying hues of dark blue, green, and black.

These notebooks contained the first stories he had written as an author. These stories had never been published, and Vincent never allowed anyone to read them. They would have made him quite a bit of money, he was sure, but his journals were for his eyes only.

It had been years since he had looked at his journals. He had begun them in the ninth grade. His English teacher, Mr. Snyder, had each of his students keep a weekly journal, detailing the most significant events of their lives. He never collected them, of course. "That would completely defeat the purpose of keeping a journal," he had told the class. "But, if you write every day, your writing skills will improve drastically. And, if you need to write every day, what better topic to write about than yourself?"

The rest of the class groaned at the idea of having to write a weekly journal. Vincent was fairly certain that he was the only one that kept up with it throughout the year. His life was interesting. Tragic—but interesting. He wasn't even sure all of what he knew of it was true. His mother liked to provide him with the details of his early life, and Vincent was well aware that his mother was prone to fantasies.

He had tried to verify all he could before putting his life stories into his journals. The first page, marked "September 5, 1970," told the story of his first day in the world. Not in as much detail as Kevin Larre had written in the manuscript, but enough to make his birth seem as dramatic. He remembered his mother telling him how she almost lost him several times right after he was born.

Strangled by the umbilical cord.

Kidnapped by doctors.

Stolen by a little girl with pigtails.

Vincent still didn't know how Kevin Larre could have known such intimate facts, especially about his scars. *Could Kevin Larre be a doctor? Was he there when I was born?*

He shook the thought from his head, certain the idea was a ridiculous fabrication of his imaginative mind. He would just need to wait and hear back from Devon.

Vincent remembered the day his mother told him about the little girl with pigtails. He was thirteen, and they had lived in countless other apartments since then. He had hopped on a bus and hunted down the apartment that served as his first home. Determined to discover the truth of his childhood, he knocked on every door in the building. Tenants of the building were either overweight bald men wearing wife beaters but having no wives, old women in faded, stained floral nightgowns with breasts covering their bellybuttons, or younger women with large, fake earrings dancing from their ears and babies dangling from their chests.

Vincent wondered if his mother ever answered the door with him attached to her nipple. Unfortunately, all he learned on his quest was that residents of the building rarely stayed more than a few years. No one had ever heard of Janet Kraver.

Vincent had learned to take his mother's stories with a grain of salt. He accepted the fact that they might not all have been true. Knowing his mother, however, Vincent was fully prepared to believe that Janet had indeed left him alone in his stroller when he was four days old, inviting anyone who passed to take him away. Sometimes, he wished the little girl with pigtails had succeeded in her kidnapping pursuit. Nothing could have been worse than being raised by Janet Kraver.

Vincent's thoughts came back to the present and his mother today. Seventy-five, hunched over, and still pursuing her life dream, whatever that might be. Janet spent a lot of her time at Everly wondering where she went wrong when raising her son. She gave Vincent all she could give—her love, her devotion—and what did he give her? A one-way ticket to Everly, an assisted living facility where the only time she got out was the Sunday bus trip to church and the supermarket. She wasn't even religious, but she was willing to thank Jesus if it got her out of Everly for a few hours.

Vincent had received a letter from his mother last week detailing her new life goal. He found it odd that Janet sometimes forgot she was mad at him long enough to write him another convoluted letter. Apparently, she now wanted to be a hair dresser. Many of the residents at Everly looked exactly the same with short, stark white hair. She made special note of the number of women who looked like men with more hair protruding from their chins than from their heads.

The staff at Everly provided a challenge to Janet's realization of her inner beautician. She got herself into trouble when she had dyed her roommate's hair brown with coffee she took from the dining room. The staff finally sensed something was askew with Rosaline's hair when she was being followed all day by a swarm of flies. Vincent started to feel the same depression sneaking up on him that he always felt when trying to figure out the truth of his life. It was this depression that kept him from unlocking the bottom drawer of his desk for so many years. He knew now, however, that keeping his journals shut up would not settle his anxiety this time around. Kevin Larre had somehow managed to unlock Vincent's past and had sent it to him in an envelope along with his baby picture.

Kevin Larre knew things about Vincent. And, the one thing about Vincent that *everyone* was aware of was his love of mysteries. Vincent thought about the brilliance of this new, unknown author. *Kraver*, a biography of the mystery writer Vincent Kraver, written by mystery author Kevin Larre. Vincent's anxiety persisted, but rather than being anxious about his past, he was anxious about the future writing of Kevin Larre. He sincerely hoped to receive more of the manuscript, and soon.

His wish was granted as he walked into his house and saw an envelope on the table outside his office with a picture of the five-year-old Vincent glued to the corner.

SIX

Playground Blues

Vincent sat Indian-style under the jungle gym watching and listening to the other children—happy children. The sounds of feet scampering across the rickety bridge seemed to never end. Neither did the sound of laughter. Vincent had never laughed like the other children he heard. It wasn't fair, but he had learned long ago that life was rarely fair, especially to him.

He didn't know how much time he had spent at the playground. He came here every day, as often as he could to get away from the unpleasant sounds of his home. It wasn't even his home or his mother's. It was Carson's. Carson was the man his mother had been spending most of her time with lately. The only reason Vincent could possibly think of for his mom to be with someone like Carson was that he shared his home with them.

That was really the only reason Janet Kraver was ever with someone. It was either get a boyfriend or find a new bridge to sleep under that night.

Other than the fact he was nice enough to give them a place to stay, Carson treated Janet and Vincent like they were lower than dirt. Janet did everything he asked her to do.

Come to think of it, he didn't even ask her to do anything. He simply gave her an order and expected it to be obeyed. And, of course, Vincent was often included in his mother's chores.

The worst chore was laundry. Every Sunday was laundry day. Since there was no laundry room in their building, Janet and Vincent had to walk nine blocks to the nearest laundromat. And, since he was obsessed with his appearance, Carson usually changed his outfit twice a day. This turned one week of laundry into what felt like two or three weeks' worth.

Vincent never learned what Carson did for a living. All he knew was it involved looking good every day. He wore tight fitted shirts that showed off his impressive pectoral and abdominal muscles. He made sure Janet ironed every piece of clothing he planned to wear the next day. He even expected his underwear to be wrinkle-free.

Carson's shoes always had to be spotless. Vincent was given the exquisite job of shining his shoes. He hated that Carson made him wash his clothes, and he hated that his mom didn't stand up to him. The bruises that often appeared around his mother's eyes and on her arms made him think twice about talking back.

He watched his mother cry while she cleaned the bathroom, dusted the furniture, and picked up Carson's dirty underwear. Just as quickly as her tears came, her smile and

laughter came back when he handed her a weekly allowance. Vincent always thought his mother was more like Carson's maid than his girlfriend. She had to earn a spot in his house. If she didn't do her chores, she was beaten or starved. Often times it was both. It was also pretty common for Vincent to be included in his mother's punishments, which is why he came to the playground so often by himself.

Vincent's attention was brought back to the playground when he heard a large group of kids screaming. He peered out from his hiding spot and saw a bunch of boys and girls a few years older than him coming together in a group. The way they acted around each other showed this wasn't the first time they all played together.

Vincent wished more than anything that he could be a part of that group. Never had Vincent been part of anything remotely fun. The only group activity he ever was asked to join in was the Sunday laundry. By asked, he of course meant demanded. And, by group, he meant him and his mom alone doing chores without any assistance from his mom's boyfriend.

Vincent observed the swarm of kids. They huddled in a tight pack before dispersing quickly in all directions. They all screamed as if the slightest silence would ruin the game. After the group took off, Vincent saw one boy remaining where the group had been. His hands covered his eyes and Vincent could

hear him counting loudly. By the time he reached twenty, all the other kids had found places to hide around the playground.

"Ready or not, here I come!" the eager boy shouted. He sprinted to a cluster of trees on the other side of the park. As he rushed towards the trees, a bunch of kids emerged like a flock of birds. They scattered to find new hiding spots. Many ran to hold onto the swing set pole they had designated as base.

Vincent watched the boy chasing everyone run in a direction away from the jungle gym when a girl joined him underneath it. Her face was flushed and she panted as if she had just run a marathon.

"Oh, hi," she said when she noticed Vincent. "Mind if I hide here?"

"That's fine." Vincent looked the girl up and down. Her green tee-shirt hung loose over her blue jeans. She wore sneakers of the same color. Her mass of blond hair was gathered in a messy bun on top of her head. Some strands stuck to her forehead as beads of sweat formed across her temple.

"I'm Amber by the way," the girl said without taking her eyes away from her surroundings.

"I'm Vincent," he replied. After a few minutes of Amber catching her breath, Vincent tried to speak to her. "What are you guys playing?"

Amber was still out of breath. "Tag."

"What's tag?"

Amber looked at Vincent as if he'd just asked her what gender she was. "You've never heard of tag?"

"No," Vincent responded sheepishly.

"It's a game where someone named 'It' chases you. If 'It' tags you, you become 'It'."

"What's the point of the game?"

"To not get tagged."

After considering Amber's description of the game, Vincent decided tag sounded like fun. "Can I play?"

"Well," Amber answered slowly, looking Vincent up and down for the first time. "It's really more for older kids. How old are you?"

"Five."

"Well, I'm eight, and I'm the youngest in the group. You're too young. Maybe in a couple years."

Vincent was about to protest when Amber ran off. "Gotta go," she whispered quickly before ditching him.

He felt stupid for having asked if he could join in their game. No one ever approached him and asked if he wanted to play. His own mother never even came to the park with him.

True, Carson pretty much owned her and ordered her to do whatever he wanted, but that didn't mean she couldn't find a part of her day to spend with her son, right? Vincent leaned back in his hiding place to wallow in self-pity.

Sometimes, Vincent wondered if his mother loved him or saw him as a nuisance. He already knew how his father had felt. He'd never even met the man, but at least his feelings were clear. Janet Kraver was often difficult to read. There were times when Janet seemed like she did everything she could for her love of Vincent. She tried her best to keep a roof over his head, even enduring severe beatings from Carson for forgetting to order his ham and turkey sandwich without tomatoes or for coming back from the laundromat with a sock missing.

There were other times, however, when Vincent felt his mother didn't care if he existed. Whenever Carson would focus his anger on Vincent's five-year-old frame, Janet never stepped in to defend him. Normally, a mother would do everything in her power to protect her child, but not Janet Kraver. She let Carson beat him and didn't interfere either because she was afraid or because she didn't care. Vincent had a strong feeling it was the latter, especially when she came up to him after a brutal chastisement and said something like, "Maybe next time you'll do a better job," or, "Maybe you'll listen from now on."

And then there was the obvious fact that he was here at the playground now, alone. He was probably the only five-year-old who was forced to go out by himself to feel safer. Most moms took great joy in bringing their children to the park. The only places Vincent's mom ever brought him to were the laundromat, the supermarket, or any place where she could use his help getting errands done.

Before he could think any more about his sad life, new sounds caught his attention. It was the sound of a child laughing. He peeked out to find the laughter's source and found a boy about his age sitting in the sandbox. He looked content even though he was playing by himself. He was wearing a bright red shirt with a looming dragon hovering in the center, wings spread and mouth agape. A trail of smoke came from its mouth indicating its power to breathe fire. The fire that came from its mouth probably matched the fire in its eyes.

Vincent was afraid of being rejected by this boy the same way he was rejected by Amber, so he kept his distance. His urge to go over and help him build castles in the sand, however, only grew as he continued to observe him.

He wasn't sure how long he had been looking at the other child. Vincent glanced around and was surprised to see the crowd thinning. The older group of kids that was playing

tag had dispersed a while ago. The temperature dropped indicating it would be a cool evening. As much as he hated the thought, Vincent knew it was time for him to go home.

He crawled out from beneath the jungle gym on his hands and knees. He stood up and swiped at the sand that had caked on the seat of his pants. Carson would be angry if Vincent tracked sand into the apartment. He had the bruise on his back to prove it.

While checking to make sure he got every speck of sand off, he heard a light, cheery voice floating through the air. He glanced up and saw a woman gesturing towards the boy he had been watching. The woman, obviously the boy's mother, was wearing a pair of loose jeans and an oversized sweatshirt with UCLA scrawled across it. Vincent took an educated guess that the sweatshirt originally belonged to the man sitting next to the woman and it somehow made its way into her closet.

"Let's go, Harry," the mother said. "It's almost time for dinner."

"I'm not done," answered Harry. He proceeded to refill his pail with more sand.

"Come on. Listen to your mother." Harry's father walked towards him. "You don't want to miss your favorite show, do you?"

“Oh yeah,” said Harry with delight. Vincent wondered what Harry’s favorite show was. He’d love to be able to go home with them to find out.

A pain grew in Vincent’s chest as he watched the threesome gather up their belongings to head home. He never knew his own father, and his mother certainly never showed him the same affection that Harry’s mother showed her son.

Without realizing it, Vincent started crying over what he didn’t have. His body trembled as he tried to fight back the persistent tears. He had to end the crying before going home. If there was one thing Carson despised more than sand being tracked into the house, it was Vincent’s tears. There were so many things that made Carson angry.

Vincent plodded over to the bench where Harry’s parents had been a few seconds ago. He sat there until he had his emotions under control. By the time he was ready to leave, Harry and his parents were out of sight. They were probably heading to a happy home—a home that didn’t bruise Harry’s body or spirit.

As the sky grew dark, Vincent lifted himself from the bench and began his trek to Carson’s apartment. It was only a few blocks, but for a five-year-old it could feel like a few miles. Everyone he passed would give him an awkward look as if to say, “What are you doing out by yourself?” Vincent

sometimes wished someone would take advantage of the little boy walking by himself. Maybe, he could be whisked away into a different life—a better life.

Unfortunately, Vincent's dreams of being kidnapped went unfulfilled. It seemed like he would need to stick with Janet Kraver for better or for worse.

Vincent rounded the corner and headed towards the entrance of Carson's apartment building. He stood on his tiptoes to push the button that would buzz him in.

"Who is it?" came his mother's raspy voice.

"It's me," Vincent replied.

"Who?"

Vincent rolled his eyes. "Vincent. Let me in."

"Oh, Vincent. Come on in." It was hard to tell over the intercom, but it sounded like his mother had been crying.

As he climbed the stairs, Vincent heard yelling and scuffling. He immediately knew his mother and Carson were having another brawl and considered turning around and heading back down the stairs. Janet had already buzzed him in, however, so he continued his ascent into hell.

The door to the apartment was slightly ajar. When Vincent tried to push the door open, he noticed a duffle bag blocking it from opening completely.

"Let's go!" Carson yelled. "I said whatever fits into that bag. I think that's being generous enough."

Janet's face was streaked with tears. "I can't fit all my clothes and Vincent's clothes into one bag." She ran around the room grabbing anything she thought she could save.

Carson continued to scream at Vincent's mother. "And who the fuck do you think paid for all your clothes, huh? You're lucky I don't burn everything."

Vincent remained glued to his spot by the door, too afraid to move any further into the apartment.

Before he could continue his tirade, Carson's cell phone rang. "What? Now? I'm busy. He can't handle that shit by himself? Fine, I'll be there in fifteen." Carson closed the phone violently. Then, he spoke to Janet with a definite threat in his voice. "When I get back later, I want you and your little brat gone, for good."

Turning towards the door, Carson spotted Vincent for the first time since he got home. "Speaking of little brat." Carson walked over to Vincent and grabbed him by the collar. The smell of beer and tacos filled his nostrils as Carson leaned his face close to Vincent's. "Help the bitch pack before she forgets to pack any of your shit. Women only think about themselves. Just a bit of manly advice for you in case you ever manage to grow a pair."

The sound of Carson's footsteps faded as he went down the stairs, but the sound of Vincent's heart beating continued well after he was gone.

"I'm sorry, sweetie." Vincent looked at his mother's face. It had acquired a few more bruises since that morning. "Will you ever forgive me?" Janet held out her arms to him.

All Vincent could think of was how many times his mother had said those exact words to him. No longer able to keep his emotions at bay, he ran past his mother into the bathroom, slammed the door, and let the tears fall freely.

SEVEN

Other than feeling completely creeped out after reading about his five-year-old self, Vincent woke up the next morning in a slightly better mood than he'd been in for the past several days. Just as he suspected, Lillian had forgiven him, or at least chosen to forget about the fights they recently had been having. His advances toward her in the bedroom were ignored. At least he was allowed back into his own bed, which was a vast improvement after two nights on the pullout couch in his office.

He glanced at the clock and saw it was 7:23 am. He knew Lillian would be downstairs making breakfast for Neil and Susan. His kids were probably the only ones who ate breakfast before noon thanks to their top chef mother.

Vincent found his slippers next to his bed and trudged to the bathroom. A fleeting look in the mirror revealed a tired looking man who had overcome many trials and tribulations in his life. And he had, hadn't he? Kevin Larre seemed to be intent on reminding him through his manuscript.

The memories Kevin Larre excavated from Vincent's hidden past were supposed to stay that way—hidden. Vincent had come a long way since being the poor boy forced to wash an older man's underwear to avoid a beating. Any recollection Vincent had of being punched, kicked, and starved had been successfully buried in a part of his brain that he intended to keep sealed forever. The only other time since his childhood that Vincent had thought about Carson was when he wrote about him in his journal. Now, after nearly forty years of forgetting his painful upbringing, Kevin Larre was forcing Vincent to face everything once more.

Vincent turned on the faucet and let the water run warm before splashing it on his face. He risked another glance in the mirror but the reflection was the same. His skin was slightly wrinkled around his continually graying eyes. After everything he'd been through, Vincent liked to think they were filled with more wisdom.

The phone rang and Vincent pulled his face away from his reflection. After two rings, the phone was silent. He figured Lillian answered it. He looked back at himself and tried to imagine the little boy in the photo that was glued to the envelope he had received. Much had changed over fifty years, but the eyes kept their mystery. They had always been observant, waiting for anything interesting to add to a lifetime of memories.

Unfortunately, almost all of Vincent's memories were unpleasant. Why was Kevin Larre so intent on rudely shoving them back in his face? Vincent had never even heard of the man, yet this writer knew so much about Vincent. Kevin Larre had to be someone close to him. What was Vincent missing? He had been convinced that nothing could puzzle him. This feeling of utter confusion was very new and disturbing.

No matter how much he learned over the years, Vincent still couldn't understand why his mother spent so much time with Carson. There was the fact that he gave them a place to stay when they had nowhere else to go. But, his rules for living with him had made his apartment feel more like a dictatorship than a home.

If Janet and Vincent didn't work, they weren't fed. They weren't given their weekly allowance. Of course, the weekly allowance wasn't such a huge concern for little Vincent. He didn't understand the concept of money back then. Hell, he barely understood it now. There were other consequences for breaking Carson's rules, however – painful consequences.

Kevin Larre had been correct when it came to tracking sand into the house. Carson demanded everything in his life be spotless, especially his apartment. He would say that his line of business was completely reliant on him keeping up a certain appearances. Anyone who hindered that appearance, as Vincent and his mother so often did, would be punished.

Carson never told Vincent exactly what he did for a living. He figured it must be important because he was always conducting business meetings in his apartment. Whenever these meetings would take place, Vincent and Janet had been locked in the bedroom. Their presence would have probably marred his perfectly immaculate apartment.

He knew now what Carson had done. He was a pimp. His business meetings involved discussing the sale of his women whom he had complete control over. Sometimes, Vincent thought about how lucky his mother was since she didn't become one of his girls for sale. She remained in his apartment as the maid and occasional sex toy. Vincent also knew they were lucky that Carson had gotten fed up with them and threw them out of his apartment. As terrible as it was on the streets, who knows where he'd be today if he remained in the care of a pimp?

Vincent was proud of all he had accomplished in his life. He saw himself as the quintessential success story that would enthrall other people. He had never, however, planned to actually make his life story known to the public. He kept his memories under lock and key and tried to forget those people like Carson who made his life treacherous.

He'd been successful thus far. Vincent was pissed that Kevin Larre had been able to dig up these intimate details of his past. He was pissed that Kevin Larre had the gall to put these memories on paper and deliver them to him. Vincent was even more pissed that he still didn't have a clue as to the identity of Kevin Larre. What pissed Vincent off the most, however, was how much he was enjoying the mystery Kevin Larre was creating for him.

Vincent walked into the kitchen in his robe and slippers. He was looking forward to a bacon cheese omelet even though he knew Lillian would object. His doctor made it clear to them that bacon, among other things, must be cut from his diet. Though he never liked being told what to do or how to live his life, Vincent followed his doctor's orders very loosely.

He walked up behind Lillian who was busy at the stove, gave her a peck on the cheek and placed his order. Lillian gave him a frustrated look.

"What?" he asked.

Lillian shrugged her shoulders. "If you so desperately want that heart attack, the bacon's in the fridge."

"With the way you cook, I'd gladly welcome a heart attack." Vincent went to retrieve the bacon from the refrigerator and was pleased to see Lillian had bought him his milk.

"Devon called this morning," Lillian said as he handed her the ingredients for his omelet.

"Really? What did he want?"

"He wanted to remind you that you have a book signing in Montclair today."

"Oh right. I completely forgot."

"Yeah, he figured you would," Lillian replied. "He also said he's not feeling well and can't make it, so you'll need to find another ride."

Vincent sat down hard into a chair at the table. "Just leave it to my agent to make my life more difficult. Can I take your car today? The Mercedes people seem to be taking their own sweet-ass time with mine."

"Not today," answered Lillian. "I'm working at the restaurant from four until midnight. And, I have errands to run before that."

"Damn." Vincent rubbed his eyes as he tried to come up with a solution.

"Why don't you take Neil's car?" Lillian suggested. "I'm sure he won't mind."

"That's a good idea," Vincent said. "Even if he does mind, I'm the one who pays for it."

"You should still ask him to borrow it rather than just take it. Be respectful to your son."

"I'm not gonna ask Neil for something that technically isn't his."

"You're not gonna ask me for what?" Neil came into the kitchen still half asleep.

Lillian gave Vincent a sharp look before he responded. He chose his words carefully so as not to upset his wife and son. "If you don't mind, I would very much appreciate the use of your car today to get to my book signing since mine is still under maintenance." He topped off his performance with a cheesy smile.

The sarcasm in Neil's response was just as blatant as his father's had been. "Well, since you asked me so nicely, I guess I can let you borrow it for a day." His cheesy smile was an exact replica of Vincent's.

"Don't be a wiseass," said Vincent.

"What? You can be a wiseass but I can't? Where's the logic in that?"

"The logic is I'm old enough and successful enough to be a wiseass. You're just a teenager who has everything handed to you on a silver platter. Learn to be grateful for once."

"You know what?" Neil was clearly angry now. "I changed my mind. You can't borrow my car. You can walk to your damn book signing."

"Or, you could walk to school…" Vincent was cut off by Lillian slamming his plate down on the table in front of him.

"How about you eat your heart attack omelet in silence and shower so you can get the kids to school on time?"

"I'm not hungry," said Neil as he turned to leave the kitchen. "I'll be in my room."

Vincent and Lillian stared at each other in silence as their son stomped up the steps and slammed the door to his room.

"When's the last time you actually had a pleasant conversation with him?" Lillian asked.

"You ask me that like I'm the one who starts the fights," Vincent replied.

"Well you talk to him like he's a five-year-old. He's seventeen. It's time you started treating Neil with some respect."

"I can't treat him with respect until he acts more responsible."

"It's not like you're setting a very good example."

Vincent put his fork down mid-bite. "What's that supposed to mean?"

Lillian leaned against the counter and crossed her arms. "It means that nine times out of ten, you have someone else do things for you rather than taking care of things yourself."

"That's not true," said Vincent defensively.

"It absolutely *is* true," Lillian countered. "Like the other day with the milk. You made me go out and get it instead of getting it yourself. Do you have any idea how pathetic that is?"

"I was busy."

"So was I."

Vincent stared down at his half-eaten breakfast, annoyed that the milk had somehow become the center of their argument once again.

"And, what about your Epipen?" asked Lillian. "Did you get that refilled yet? Or, are you waiting for me to do that too?"

He knew it was dangerous to not get his epinephrine refilled. Afterall, it could mean the difference between life and death should he ever ingest a peanut. But, he'd been very careful and only had to give himself the shot twice over the past few years. He kept one in his desk in his office. He'd get around to refilling it eventually and wished Lillian would stop nagging him about it.

"I'll get it filled on the way back from the signing today."

"Sure you will," said Lillian as she tossed pans into the sink. Vincent decided he wasn't hungry anymore and left the rest of his heart attack omelet on the table for Lillian to clean up. If she truly thought he was irresponsible, he didn't want to be rude and prove her wrong.

EIGHT

"Are you even listening to what I'm saying?" asked Neil.

Vincent looked to his right where Neil was sitting in the passenger's seat. "Yeah, I'm listening. What time do you need to be picked up?"

"Like I just said when you obviously weren't listening," said Neil, "I need to get picked up at four."

Neil was right about Vincent not paying attention. He had been preoccupied with his fight with Lillian earlier that morning as well as the book signing. He had no idea how to get to Montclair and hoped his son's GPS could show him the way.

"I don't think I'll be able to get back until around four-thirty. Can you find a place to hang out until then?"

"Yeah, we can hang out in the gym and watch the girls' basketball team practice," came a voice from the backseat. Vincent glanced in the rearview mirror and saw Neil's best friend, Justin, smirking.

Susan, who occupied the seat next to Justin, gave him a disgusted look. "You're such a pervert," she said.

"Only when thinking about you," Justin answered bouncing his eyebrows. Vincent tightened his grip on the steering wheel.

Other than being a pervert, Vincent knew Justin had a reputation for being a huge flirt.

"You seem to forget that my dad is in the car today," said Susan.

"Oh, that's right," Justin replied without the slightest hint of concern. "Sorry, Mr. Kraver. I didn't mean what I just said. I only have the utmost respect for your daughter." Neil let out a snicker at this remark and Susan stared out her window with a sulky look on her face.

"That's good to know," Vincent answered. He chose not to carry on the conversation any further. Vincent was not about to evaluate how teenagers conducted themselves nowadays. They were nothing but disrespectful and deliberately did everything in their power to make their parents' lives as difficult as possible.

Justin was especially disrespectful. He always seemed to make himself comfortable in Vincent's home. He could be found hanging out in Neil's room, even when Neil wasn't home, or sprawled on the couch eating leftovers that Vincent had planned to have the next day for lunch. It had taken a lot of convincing from Lillian to not permanently close the door on Neil's friend. According to her, Justin helped keep Neil from stressing too much over his school work and college applications. Neil had always been prone to anxiety attacks, and kicking out his best friend wouldn't solve any problems. That didn't keep Vincent from imagining Justin being tossed out one of the fourth story windows.

Vincent turned his attention to Susan. "Are you gonna need a ride home too?"

"No. I have track practice until five and then I'll get a ride home with Emily."

"Is she your hot friend?"

Vincent wondered if Justin ever knew when to keep his comments to himself.

"Whether she's hot or not, she thinks you're a dick," replied Susan. This time it was Vincent who snickered.

Vincent pulled up to the front of the high school to let Neil, Susan, and Justin out. "I'll see you at four-thirty," he called out before Neil closed the door. As his children climbed the steps to Morris High, Vincent focused on the GPS and tried to figure out how to get to his book signing.

After numerous wrong turns and driving through three wrong towns, Vincent finally arrived twenty minutes late to the book signing. *So much for GPS*, he thought to himself as he lumbered out of the car.

"Hey, Sharla."

"Hey, Vincent." Sharla looked at her watch and then back up at Vincent.

"I know I'm a little late. Took longer than I thought to get here." Vincent glanced around the room and saw that the bookstore was already crowded with fans holding copies of his book.

"Looking forward to this?" asked Sharla.

"Don't I always?"

Sharla smiled at Vincent's sarcasm. "At least you have a sense of humor."

Vincent visited the men's room as he did before every signing. He knew he'd be sitting for hours. The crowd was already out the door and the line would only grow longer as time went on.

After checking his appearance in the mirror, Vincent returned to the table where he'd be signing. It had a cup filled with pens, and there were several water bottles lined up for him. Sharla was already partway down the line with her post-its and Sharpie.

As he sat down, Vincent picked up a pen and prepared for the first guest. He noticed the first person in line had three copies of *Quiet Thunder* even though he had a policy of only one autograph per person. On the other hand, Vincent admired her long blond hair, large green eyes, and trim waist. Maybe he'd make an exception to his "one per customer" rule just this one time.

The woman walked up to the table and was about to speak when Vincent's attention was suddenly pulled away from her. A chill crept up his spine when he saw a man standing outside the window of the bookstore staring at him. With his dark clothes, black shaggy hair and dark sunglasses, Vincent recognized him right away as the mysterious stranger who approached him after his book signing only three days ago. The corners of the man's mouth curved up in a slight smile when Vincent looked at him. After what must have only been a few seconds and a tiny wave, the dark man took off.

Vincent stood up quickly, knocking the table forward and surprising the blond woman. He ran towards the exit of the store. Many pairs of eyes followed him as he rushed past his line of fans. He barely heard Sharla call his name as he was so focused on catching up to the elusive man who smiled at him through the window.

After managing to push his way out of the store, Vincent ran in the direction the dark man had gone. He stopped at a corner and looked in all directions but saw no trace of him. Feeling completely defeated, Vincent walked back to the bookstore. He made sure not to meet anyone's inquisitive gaze. It was no one's business why he ran out of the store like a lunatic.

"It's so nice to finally meet you," said the pretty blond woman with three books after Vincent settled himself behind the table.

"It's nice to meet you too," he answered without looking up. He signed one book before handing all three back to her. "I can only sign one per customer. Thanks for coming."

The hours of the book signing passed by even slower than usual. Vincent knew the first time he met the dark stranger that there was something slightly off about him. He wondered why he came to two of his signings. He had fans in the past who came to multiple signings, but never for the same book.

And besides, this man definitely did not seem like a fan. He didn't talk to him except to tell him that he was his biggest fan, clearly being sarcastic since he didn't want an autograph. What had that been about?

It seemed all the stranger intended to do was create a sense of unease in the author and disappear as quickly as possible. Well, if that was truly his intent, he had done a very good job. Vincent had never flown out of his chair as quickly as he had today when the dark stranger waved at him through the store window.

By the time the last customer left, Vincent felt his usual sense of fatigue and soreness after hours of sitting and signing. Since Devon wasn't there, Vincent took some time to talk to the store owner before saying goodbye to Sharla and finally heading to his car.

After sitting in the driver's seat for a few minutes, Vincent put the key into the ignition, sat back and let out a long sigh. He was still frustrated that he didn't catch up to the man in the dark clothes. He rubbed his sore hand and did some neck rolls to get rid of the stiffness before his long drive home.

As he went to put the car in gear, he saw it. The envelope with his seventh grade picture glued to the corner was laying on the passenger's seat begging to be ripped open.

NINE

Middle School Crisis

Vincent walked up the concrete steps to the school that would hopefully be his last until high school. Seventh grade was usually a hard year for any teenager, but entering in the middle of February didn't ease any of his adolescent tension. After deciding she was bored with her life selling detergent over the phone, Vincent's mother packed up their belongings and embarked on a new life for them.

The principal's office wasn't unlike every other one he'd been in. The office secretary glanced up for an instant before returning to the important phone conversation. Something about a mother running late with her child and asking for her son to not be marked tardy. Noticing that getting to him wasn't the most pressing matter, Vincent took a seat on one of the ripped leather chairs found at the side of the office.

As the first bell sounded, the secretary finally looked at Vincent with a polite smile.

"Did you need something?"

Gee, lady, how'd you guess? Vincent didn't state this out loud as he was trying not to get into any trouble on his very first day.

"This is my first day, and I don't know where to go."

"What's your name, son?" the secretary asked as she pulled a thick, blue binder from under the desk.

"Vincent Kraver."

The secretary, Debbie—according to the nameplate in front of her— flipped through the enormous binder. "Vincent Kraver, seventh grade, homeroom 201. Did you receive your schedule in the mail?"

"No, ma'am."

"Okay. Let me just print one out for you, then I'll walk you to your first class. You can just have someone from each of your classes point you to your next one." Vincent waited patiently as Debbie struggled with the printer. Every time she hit print, the paper would jam up.

"Sorry, we just got this thing. I'm not quite sure how to use it. I miss my typewriter."

It was as if everything, even machinery, was trying to keep Vincent from advancing to the next point in his life, wherever that may be.

"Okay, follow me," said Debbie. Her black leather shoes clicked with each step, echoing through the now empty hallways – hallways that would soon be bustling with teenagers rushing to get to their first period classes within the four minutes between bells. Vincent took in the smell of lingering

perfume, probably worn by some fifth grade girl hoping to catch the attention of the eighth-grade jocks. Two rows of jungle green lockers lined the endless halls. Vincent was sure wild animals were lurking behind every corner, waiting to devour him.

"Here we are." Debbie pointed to a door marked "201" before turning on her heel and heading back the way they came. "Just tell Mr. Weinbeck you're new so you won't be marked late," she called over her shoulder. Vincent shook his head as he wondered why adults never looked him straight in the eye when addressing him. They were always in a rush to get somewhere more important.

Straightening his back and hoping to look less nervous than he felt, Vincent walked through the door into the room full of his new classmates. His first glance around the room told him everyone was normal. No one looked evil or ready to jump him as soon as the final bell rang. But, Vincent had been through enough school systems and disappointments to know looks could be deceiving.

"Yes?" said a tall thin man whom Vincent assumed to be Mr. Weinbeck.

"Vincent Kraver, sir. I was told to tell you it's my first day and not to mark me late."

"Another student? You've got to be kidding me." Mr. Weinbeck let out a heavy sigh, as if his words didn't sting Vincent enough. "I don't know where they expect me to put you. This room is already overcrowded as it is." Vincent had to agree that the room was very stuffy. A quick count showed there to be thirty-one students already. Thirty-one students and not a desk to spare. "You can just stand in the back for today and I'll try and get a desk for you by tomorrow."

Vincent walked to the far side by the windows and made his way to the back of the classroom. Backpacks and purses filled the aisles, tripping him as he passed each desk. He made sure to avoid eye contact, although he was able to take in some of the students as he passed by. One girl, sitting in the front by the windows, was doodling on a page in her already filled notebook. He wasn't surprised that some of the drawings looked exactly like the artwork his mother sold on the street when he was a baby.

Another student was already asleep at his desk, head rolled back, mouth open, breathing in the chalk infested air. Vincent smirked as a boy two rows back attempted to throw bits of paper in the snoozer's parted lips.

When he finally reached the back of the room, Vincent decided to read over his new class schedule. Geometry, English, Physical Education, Social Studies, Science, Woodshop, Study Hall, Latin. He grimaced when he read

Latin. He didn't know he had to take a language when he came here, and of all the language choices, he certainly wouldn't have chosen a dead one to study. He would have to make an appointment with his guidance counselor to get that changed.

"Hey, you have math the same time I do." Vincent looked to his right to see the source of whomever interrupted his thoughts. His eyes fell upon a blond boy with a face dotted by freckles and acne. Vincent immediately pegged him as an outcast who tried to befriend the new kid whenever possible since the new kid wasn't likely to have any other friends yet.

"Okay," was all Vincent could think to say to this new face.

"I can show you where it is if you want. This place is pretty big."

"Okay," Vincent said again.

"You don't say much, do you?"

"No."

The boy looked around the room and bounced on his toes as he let the awkward silence sink in between them. "I'm Chris."

"Vincent."

Chris nodded slightly before returning to his seat a few feet from Vincent.

The bell rang less than a minute later, and the volume in the room seemed to grow exponentially with voices and shuffling feat. Vincent waited until everyone else exited the room before making his way into the crowded hallway. He felt his heart rate increase as it often did when he was in large, unruly crowds.

"Hey, Vinny! Over here!" Vincent looked over and was actually relieved to see Chris waving him down.

"I hate being called Vinny," he said as he approached Chris through the mass of students.

"Sorry, man," Chris replied. "I was just testing the waters. Trying to see what I could call you, now that we're friends and all."

"Vincent is fine," Vincent replied, accepting Chris as his friend at this new school. He decided a friend wouldn't be too bad a start on his first day, even if it was the class nerd. "So, you have geometry now too?"

"Yup, with Ms. Green."

Vincent looked down skeptically at his schedule. "This says I have Mrs. Elbridge."

Chris smiled, happy for a set of new ears to share the gossip with. "She's getting a divorce. She was married to Mr. Elbridge forever, but they just decided to call it quits recently."

"How do you know?" asked Vincent.

"Good news travels fast, especially about Mr. Elbridge."

"Why? Who's Mr. Elbridge?" Vincent was ashamed at himself for being curious.

Chris pointed down to Vincent's schedule. "The science teacher." Vincent thought about how awkward it would be to work in the same building as an ex-spouse, especially when the building was swarming with gossipy teenagers who had nothing better to do than discuss the tragedies of other people's lives.

Vincent carried on the conversation as he and Chris wound their way through the maze of students. "So, how do you know about them splitting up? Did they fight in the hallway or something?"

"No," said Chris. "But, it has been confirmed by several reliable sources that Mr. Elbridge was having an affair with Miss Philips, the drama teacher."

"Reliable sources?"

"They work for the school newspaper so they're good at finding stuff out."

"I wouldn't be so sure."

Chris shrugged his shoulders. "Plus, Mrs. Elbridge told all her students to call her Ms. Green from now on. So, that kind of gave it away."

"It gave away the divorce, not the affair."

"Whether it's true or not, I'm just trying to clue you in to the main events of the school so you're not completely out of the loop. You'll thank me later."

"I'm sure I will."

Vincent and Chris entered the classroom of Ms. Green just in time for the bell to ring. "See you after class," said Chris as he made his way across the room to his seat. Vincent introduced himself to his recently divorced geometry teacher before the class began, once again finding himself without a desk.

After two weeks, Vincent was able to adjust to his new schedule at his new school in his new town. Every morning, he would grab the granola bar and two dollars his mom left on the counter the night before. Janet never woke up early when she didn't have to be anywhere. Vincent always wondered what she did for money. It isn't like the two dollars he got

every day came from nowhere. But, when he noticed men's shoes appearing in the living room or bathroom, he decided to keep his curiosity to himself and go with the flow.

Vincent walked to school every day. He wasn't very comfortable on buses—too many students making too much noise for his comfort level. He also found that Chris's house was on the way to school. Since Chris's house was only a few blocks from the school, there wasn't a bus to pick him up, so he was forced to walk every day as well. Vincent found that he was rather fond of Chris, and even let Chris call him Vinny.

During his walk to school one day, Vincent was reading The Hobbit, by J.R.R. Tolkien for his English class. His mom had kept him up the night before asking for his help picking out an outfit for her job interview the next day, and he hadn't had time to read it.

"Hey, Vinny! Wait up!"

Vincent hadn't even noticed that he passed Chris's house. He found himself engrossed in the language of the book just as he did with many of the books he read.

"Sorry, I didn't see where I was."

"How can you read and walk at the same time? I can barely chew gum and walk." Vincent didn't have a hard time believing that about his friend.

"I don't know," he replied. "I guess it's like sleepwalking. Your body knows where to go while your mind is in a completely other place."

Chris took the book from Vincent. "Let me summarize this for you. Bilbo Baggins lives a humdrum hobbit life, and then goes off with some dwarves to steal from a dragon and succeeds. The end."

"I think it's a little more complicated than that," said Vincent as he took the book back and flipped to the page he was on.

Chris rolled his eyes. "Just trying to help out, man." Vincent walked the rest of the way with his head in his book while Chris yammered on about how his sister kept him up till all hours of the night singing and preparing a monologue for her audition in the school musical. Chatty people normally annoyed Vincent. But he found that as long as he didn't have to respond to everything Chris was saying, he actually enjoyed his friend's ramblings.

Vincent got home that night and was overwhelmed by the smell of garlic and tomato sauce. He walked into the kitchen, grimacing at the sight of red liquid sloshed over every surface. If his mother hadn't been standing at the stove

wearing her previously white apron, he would have been calling the police to report the bloody murder of Janet Kraver.

"How much sauce are you making?" Vincent asked while remaining in the doorway. He was afraid to enter the kitchen as it looked like a swimming pool of tomato sauce.

"Come on in and celebrate with me," Janet said to her son as sweat dripped off her brow and into the pot.

"Celebrate what?"

"I got a job!" Janet held her arms out as an invitation for an embrace. Vincent held his breath and walked through the steamy, garlic-filled air. Janet took him in a bear hug and sauce dripped all over the front of his clothes. He would have to wear his other pair of jeans the rest of the week until laundry day, unless he wanted his teachers to think he was being abused. Vincent smiled at that somewhat inviting thought.

His mother saw his smile and continued on with her good news. "So, I start tomorrow, and I decided to make us a feast to celebrate."

"A feast?" Vincent raised his eyebrows at the massive amounts of spaghetti and sauce. "It looks like you made enough to feed an army for a month."

"Yep. And, a large army at that," Janet replied with a wink. "I thought it would be appropriate considering the job I got."

Vincent waited for his mother to continue but knew she wouldn't unless he prompted her. "And, what job would that be?" He opened the refrigerator and grabbed a soft drink. Was there actually sauce on the shelves in the fridge? His mother certainly knew how to boggle his mind.

"I'm a chef!" his mother declared triumphantly.

Vincent closed the refrigerator door and stared at her with a look of shock glued to his face. It was a few seconds before any sound emanated from his throat.

"You're a what?"

"A chef."

"A chef?"

"Yes. How many times do I have to say it? I'm a chef. A chef!"

Vincent looked slowly around their war zone kitchen. "No offense, but what restaurant in its right mind would hire you as a chef?"

Janet's smile quickly disintegrated into a look of rage. "What's that supposed to mean? You don't think I can be a chef?"

"Mom, I can't even tell what color the kitchen tiles were before you started cooking."

"Sauce splatters. I expect to get a little dirty."

"There's sauce on the soda can. How'd you manage that? Did you cook in the fridge?"

"So I'm a little messy. Who cares? The taste is all that matters."

"Where do you work?"

Janet returned her attention to the sauce. "I'm not telling you."

"Why not?"

"Because, I don't want you coming back into my kitchen and telling me what a bad job I'm doing!"

Vincent was about to respond when he saw smoke coming from the oven.

"Um, mom?"

"I don't want to hear anymore from you. Why can't you be more supportive?"

"Mom."

"I swear, you're just like your father."

"Mom."

"You're gonna end up a bum unless you become more ambitious like me."

"Janet!"

"What?" By now the entire kitchen was filled with smoke.

"You're burning the garlic bread."

Before his mother could respond, the smoke detector went off. Janet let out a string of obscenities as she opened the windows and waved a broomstick in front of the screaming device. Vincent left the apartment leaving his mother and her noisy battle in the smoky haze.

By the time Vincent exited his room the next morning, his mother was already gone. He still wondered what restaurant owner was crazy enough to allow her to even step foot in the kitchen let alone cook for the customers. He learned over the years, however, not to dwell on his mother's antics because she never lasted long in any position anyway.

Vincent set about his normal day at school and was happy when the lunch bell rang. The food he was served at school wasn't gourmet, but then again, he had never eaten gourmet food before.

He found Chris waiting outside the cafeteria.

"Dude, science was so awesome today. My teacher was absent and the sub was so hot." Vincent listened to Chris go on about the substitute's long legs, shiny hair and advanced cup sizes. He found it amusing to hear Chris talk about parts of a woman's anatomy that he probably wouldn't be allowed to enjoy until he was forty. Still, his nerdy friend showed enthusiasm and who was Vincent to take that away from him?

"I have science next. I'll be sure to check her out," Vincent said.

"It would be hard not to," replied Chris with a wink.

They finally reached the food line and Vincent scanned the menu at the front. Along with the usual hamburgers, cheeseburgers and chicken patties, the special of the day was meatloaf, creamy mashed potatoes, and steamed baby carrots. Vincent's stomach churned and he decided a chicken patty would be the safest route.

"Well, well, well. Have you come to try some of my meatloaf?"

Vincent's head shot up from his tray to the source of the all too familiar voice. If looks could kill, Janet Kraver would have dropped dead on the spot.

"What the hell are you doing here?" asked Vincent, his voice on the edge of hysteria.

"Don't take that tone of voice with me. I'm your mother for God's sake."

A snicker came from further down the line. A group of girls huddling over their salads covered their mouths.

"That's your mom?" said one.

"You're kidding, right?" said another. The third girl just started giggling like an idiot.

Vincent leaned in towards his mother. He could feel his pulse quickening in his neck. "Seriously, why are you here?"

Janet mirrored her son and leaned in. "I told you last night about my chef job." Vincent had no clue what to say. In his head he was screaming. "So, do you want meatloaf or not?"

"I'll take some meatloaf," Chris chimed in, trying to ease the tension.

"Excellent choice, young man," said Janet, dishing out a tiny brick of meat.

Finally regaining his senses, Vincent dropped his tray, rushed through the crowded cafeteria, made his way to the bathroom, and threw up.

For the next few weeks, Vincent did his best to avoid his mother. Word spread quickly that the new lunch lady was

Vincent Kraver's mom. No matter how much he complained, Janet would not give up her new position as a hot shot chef.

"Don't be such a baby. At least, I'm paying the bills and putting food on the table."

Vincent certainly did notice the food being placed on the table every night. Hamburgers, cheeseburgers, chicken patties, and other forms of mystery meat that bore great resemblances to the food served at school found their way home.

"This looks just like the lunch line in the cafeteria," he said one night.

"I thought you liked the school food," replied Janet as she unwrapped a cheeseburger from its aluminum foil.

"Are you kidding? No one likes school food."

"Are you insulting my culinary skills?"

"I just think it's pathetic that our dinners consist of stolen cafeteria food."

"It's not stealing if it was gonna get thrown out anyway." Janet took a bite of her burger. Vincent noticed it was almost completely dried out. He was surprised it didn't disintegrate into dust particles. "I got some fries and ketchup packets too."

Vincent started to nibble on a fry when his mother jumped out of her chair. "Oh! I almost forgot. I have a date in an hour. I have to stop eating so I have room at the restaurant."

"How did you find time to meet someone?" asked Vincent, thoroughly amazed. "You spend all day in the school kitchen and most of the night smelling like you've been in a school kitchen."

Janet did a little twirl before responding. "It just so happens that I met someone at work."

Vincent's eyes widened. "At school?"

"At the vending machine."

"Who?"

Janet smiled. "You'll see." And, with another twirl she exited the kitchen.

A little over an hour passed and Vincent was convinced his mother had concocted the idea of a date to avoid cleaning the kitchen. It wouldn't be the first time Janet left a mess for him to clean up. As he turned on the kitchen faucet, he heard a sharp rap on the door. Vincent stood at the sink for a few seconds expecting his mother to come rushing out of her room. After the second knock, however, he decided his mother was

taking her own sweet time getting ready and didn't realize her date had arrived.

He opened the door after the third knock. "Good evening, Vincent."

Vincent's heart did a flip flop when he saw the man standing in the hall. "Good evening, Mr. Elbridge."

After a moment of awkward silence, Mr. Elbridge took it upon himself to continue the conversation. "Aren't you going to let me in?" Vincent stepped aside to let his science teacher into his home. He was not quite sure of the proper etiquette in this type of situation.

"Um, do you want a drink or something?"

"No thanks. Did you finish the reading for tomorrow?"

"Yeah. Good stuff." Vincent lied. He actually wasn't even aware there was an assignment.

Mr. Elbridge eyed him suspiciously. "What was the most interesting part for you?"

Vincent felt his face get hot. "Um…"

"Walter! So nice to see you!" For the first time in a long time Vincent was relieved to see his mother. He noticed she was wearing her usual first date attire. Tight black pants and a red sleeveless shirt with a deep plunging neckline that enhanced all of her curves.

Mr. Elbridge obviously liked what he saw. "Wow. You look great. Ready to go?"

"You bet," Janet responded with a bright smile.

"I'll see you tomorrow, buddy," Mr. Elbridge said to Vincent before turning to leave, his mother hanging on his arm.

Buddy? How can you call me buddy? You're my teacher! You control my grades and you're dating my mother? How can you do this? Aren't there rules against this type of behavior? Are you gonna give me a pop quiz every time my mom is a few minutes late getting ready? This is bullshit! You can't date my mom! Get the fuck out of my house you dick!

"Bye, Mr. Elbridge." Vincent decided to let his little rant stay in his head.

"So how are things going between your mom and Mr. Elbridge?"

"Shut up, Chris!" Vincent hadn't been able to get used to his mom's new fling even though a month had passed.

Chris did his best to ease Vincent's mind even though it never worked. "It's not as bad as you're letting on. I've seen them together. They seem to actually like each other."

Vincent couldn't agree with his friend's words. "Even if they like each other, why can't they think about me and how it's affecting me? It's like they do whatever they want and don't think about the fact that it's incredibly awkward for me. Everyone in school knows that my mom, the lunch lady, is dating my science teacher, who happens to be my math teacher's cheating ex-husband. And, I would say it can't get any worse, but any time I say that, it comes back and bites me in the ass."

Chris listened to Vincent continue his complaints about his mother's relationship with Mr. Elbridge until the bell dismissed them from homeroom. The walk to first period was filled with stares at Vincent that had become somewhat normal. He wished there was some underground tunnel he could take to his classes instead of having to deal with everyone's critical gaze.

Lunch had become Vincent's least favorite part of the day. He no longer went into the cafeteria. Instead, he ducked into the bathroom and ate whatever leftovers he could find in the fridge from dinner the night before. It was usually food his mother stole from the cafeteria anyway.

Geometry had become quite an ordeal for Vincent as well. Ms. Green, the former Mrs. Elbridge, was very aware of Vincent's mother and her ex-husband being an item. Luckily,

Ms. Green didn't let her anger affect the way she graded Vincent, but her attitude towards him certainly wasn't pleasant. She never called on him—barely even made eye contact. This didn't affect Vincent that much, however, since he preferred to keep to himself most of the time.

The smile Ms. Green gave him one morning was enough to make Vincent suspicious of impending news. And, news wasn't usually good for Vincent. After everyone took their seats, Ms. Green took her spot front and center to make an important announcement. "I would just like everyone to know that from now on, my name will go back to being Mrs. Elbridge."

A combined gasp sounded from around the room as all eyes turned to look at Vincent. Chris looked at him with a questioning look. It was obvious he wanted to say something to Vincent to make him feel better, but he just couldn't come up with any words. Vincent understood his friend's silence. He couldn't seem to formulate any sentences in his own head.

After the bell ending first period sounded, Chris stuck to Vincent's side. "I'm so sorry man. I have no idea what to say."

"It's alright," Vincent said. "The only thing to say is goodbye."

"What do you mean?" Chris looked perplexed by Vincent's statement.

Vincent continued. "I think I'm gonna head home now. I wanna get a head start on packing."

"Packing?"

"Yeah. I don't think I'll be coming to school here anymore. I'm surprised I was even here this long."

Chris's confusion wasn't lessened by Vincent's explanation. "I don't get it. Why do you think you're leaving?"

"Because, I know my mother. It was only a matter of time before we left here and moved on to another town."

"Just because your mom broke up with Mr. Elbridge?" Vincent nodded and held out his hand. Chris shook it before shaking his head and moving towards his next class. "It was nice knowing you."

Sure enough, Vincent walked into his home and found boxes piled everywhere. Another town, another school—another chapter of his life—had ended before it barely started.

TEN

Vincent drove home with the air conditioner on full blast. Sweat poured down the sides of his face even though he had every vent directed at him. He knew he was speeding, but he somehow hoped the faster he drove, the quicker he'd be able to get out of the nightmare that controlled his life. Of course, trying to escape one nightmare only brought on another one when he saw the lights flashing in the rearview mirror.

"Shit," he muttered as he pulled to the side of the road. Vincent didn't know if he was more annoyed that he'd be getting a ticket with a hefty fine or that this police officer was delaying him from getting home and back to his identity search for Kevin Larre.

Finding the manuscript on the front seat of his car was like a wakeup call to Vincent. Whoever Kevin Larre was, he managed to break into his locked car while he was in the book signing. Before, he was just someone who somehow knew intimate details about Vincent Kraver and wrote them down. Creepy, but not worth reporting.

Now, he was breaking into his car, a definite criminal act and much more threatening than before. Why would Kevin Larre go through so much trouble to deliver his manuscript when he could just leave it at his front door? Was it possible that Kevin Larre wanted Vincent to feel more exposed? More defenseless?

Another fact that just occurred to Vincent was he wasn't driving his usual car. His Mercedes had been in the shop now for almost a week, and Devon was the one giving him rides to and from the book signings in his crappy minivan. Whoever delivered the manuscript knew what his son's car looked like. This meant Kevin Larre was not only a threat to Vincent, but to his family as well. Vincent knew the time had come to report Kevin Larre and the manuscripts to the police.

Through his side mirror, he watched the police officer approach. Vincent knew this was the perfect opportunity to report his stalker. Maybe getting stopped for speeding was a blessing in disguise. A sign that now was the time to fulfill an obligation to protect himself and his family. Vincent felt more vulnerable since Kevin Larre managed to get the manuscript into his car while he was at his signing. Breaking and entering was certainly a crime worth reporting, right?

Vincent was also sure he knew what Kevin Larre looked like. At least he was *pretty* sure. The man in black was high on his suspect list. Granted, his suspect list was rather minimal. But, what were the odds of a sinister stranger like that showing up to two of his book signings within the same week and not being related to the manuscripts that highlighted the worst times of his life?

On the other hand, there was another part of Vincent that didn't believe the dark man had any correlation to Kevin Larre.

He had never seen him before this week. How could someone he never met be privy to such confidential facets of his life. Vincent always considered himself to be very observant, and there's no way he would have *not* noticed the man in black if he had shown up before.

His doubt that the stranger at his signing and Kevin Larre were one and the same now made Vincent think twice about reporting him to the police. He did not want to be responsible for falsely having a man arrested for…for…

For what? What would he even say to the police officer?

Hello, officer, the reason I was speeding was because there was this really creepy guy in dark clothes who showed up to my book signing and ran away from me after I ran out of the bookstore to chase him like a lunatic. I'm pretty sure he's writing mean things about me. I don't know who he is or anything about him, but can you arrest him for me? Thank you.

Before making himself look like a complete idiot, Vincent decided against reporting the threatening, peculiar, book-signing attendee and the equally disturbing Kevin Larre. Even if he knew it would sound ridiculous to others, Vincent had a very strong feeling the dark man was Kevin Larre. If he could only prove it. After all, both men showed up in his life on the same day, and Vincent did not believe in coincidences.

In every one of his novels, his main character seemed to undergo a slew of coincidental events that came together with a practical explanation in the final chapter. Nothing was ever a coincidence in a novel, and Vincent had no doubt the same set of rules could be applied to the mystery being created by Kevin Larre.

Vincent looked in his side mirror and watched as the police officer approached his car. Now was the time to decide whether or not to report Kevin Larre, and whether or not to put an end to the manuscripts that reminded Vincent of the path that brought him to where he is today…

"In a bit of a rush today, sir?"

Vincent glanced up at a young officer who looked as if he was fresh out of the academy. "No rush, officer," he responded with a pathetic smile. "Just being careless I guess."

Forty-five minutes and a three hundred dollar ticket later, Vincent made it back to his house. His stress level was still high after finding a manuscript on the front seat of the car he knows he locked before going into the signing.

Kevin Larre showed no apprehension when it came to getting his work to Vincent. He did it whenever and however he wanted. Becoming a stalker didn't seem like such a far-fetched idea for someone who was already so enthralled with his life to actually write about it. Still, it's not like someone can be considered a stalker for knowing when and where his book signings would be. If that was the case, every one of his fans could be considered a stalker. Vincent grinned at the thought of his work having such a profound effect on everyone.

Maybe Patrick has a point when he says I'm narcissistic, he thought. *Not that I'll ever tell him that. Oh well.*

Vincent marched quickly through his house toward his office. Before approaching the door, however, he stopped short and did a quick u-turn. He moved back down the hall and entered a room directly across from the kitchen. The room was sparsely furnished. In it sat a pink couch that looked almost as uncomfortable to sit on as it actually was, a wooden coffee table with gold legs and a glass cabinet filled with gold, silver, and crystal figurines. The walls were adorned with paintings that art dealers insisted every well-to-do, upscale home should have. He never bothered to learn the names of the various artists that ornamented these walls. He just gave in to the adamant voices of his wife and sales people.

He didn't come into this room often – no one did. It was the kind of room where people were afraid to go in for fear of contaminating the pristine décor. In spite of this, Vincent walked into the room today and went up to one picture of a woman wearing a big white dress and obscenely large hat while sitting in a gazebo eating a pear. Not exactly his particular taste in art, but a definite step up from whatever crap his mother tried to sell on the street when he was a baby.

After looking around to make sure no one was present, he pulled the picture off the wall. He grunted as he was reminded of the picture's weight. He laid it down on the plush carpet whose color matched the same awful pink of the uncomfortable couch.

Vincent looked at the top corner of the frame and found what he was searching for. Two spare keys—one for his office and one for the bottom drawer of his desk—were taped in their secret location should he ever misplace the originals. With a sigh of relief, Vincent replaced the picture on the wall. He was happy to know that no one had discovered them.

He remembered the last time he went to find the spare keys. It was about six months ago during the summer. Lillian's car had to get new brakes installed, and Vincent let her take his car to work. It wasn't until she rounded the corner that he realized he forgot to remove his office key. Not a big deal. He was careful to be discrete when he got the spare key from behind the "Woman Eating Pear" picture.

At least he thought he was discrete.

Who could have seen him that day? Susan was rarely home during the summer, and Neil always kept to himself in his bedroom.

Vincent went back to his office and settled himself behind his desk. He knew he had gotten nowhere in discovering who Kevin Larre was or how he was getting his information for his manuscripts. The information, after all, was in his journals, and they remained locked in his desk drawer. Vincent was sure of that. He was *pretty* sure of that.

Just to be *completely* sure, he reached into his pocket and pulled out his key ring. He found the key to unlock his drawer of journals. Vincent was nervous that they would be missing, and there was only one way to find out. He hadn't opened this drawer in years. He always preferred to keep his past locked away.

Vincent shuddered at the thought of his most prized and personal possessions in the hands of someone so intent on putting his private life on paper for Vincent, and God knows who else, to read.

Vincent pulled the bottom drawer open and glanced inside. Relief washed over him as he found each of his journals in the drawer. The thought of them missing was enough to make his heart try to escape from his chest. Vincent had no idea what he would do if he opened the drawer and found it empty.

He looked down at the journals—plain spiral notebooks whose pages had slightly yellowed with age. To the average observer, they would look like nothing special. Just the random writings of a high school student trying desperately to remember and make sense of his convoluted past. To Vincent, however, his journals were the beginnings of what became the rest of his life. He hadn't realized how much he enjoyed writing until he began journaling what he could remember of his past.

Vincent pulled a few of the notebooks out and flipped through the stiffening pages. The handwriting was equivalent to chicken scratch. Only Vincent and someone with a high level of determination would be able to decipher Vincent's stories.

After going through the first few notebooks, Vincent began to skim through the fourth one. The corners of his mouth curled up slightly because he was going against his vow to never look back at his journals. Vincent felt that the successful life he built for himself had no need to be interrupted by him going through his less than perfect childhood.

Patrick, of course, felt the exact opposite. As a psychologist, he felt that because the past made us who were are, it was important to look back and understand it. Whenever a patient came in with a problem, the first thing Patrick would ask the patient to do was to describe everything about his past, even the events that seemed irrelevant. If a woman was having a recurring nightmare, it was a painful memory that was trying to be remembered and accepted. Until the past was recognized, there could be no successful healing and closure for any of Patrick's patients.

Therefore, Patrick would be happy that Vincent was finally flipping through the pages of his history. He had said numerous times that the present and future could only be fixed by dealing with the past. Other than Vincent, Pat was the only person who knew of the journals and had encouraged him on and off over the years to sit and read them. Reading them would be in his best interest.

If Kevin Larre ever decided to make himself known, Pat would probably shake his hand for forcing Vincent to finally dive headfirst into his childhood.

Vincent paused on a page when he found Chris's name scrawled in his messy handwriting. He didn't need Kevin Larre or his journals to remind him of the friend he made in seventh grade. If it hadn't been for his mother's not so stellar dating record, Vincent was positive Chris would have remained his good friend for years, possibly a lifetime.

He thought about his young buddy and where he was today. He wondered if Chris had grown out of his dorky adolescent appearance and become a handsome adult. Had he been successful in finding a career? A wife? A home? These questions would remain unanswered thanks to Janet Kraver's ability to end all of Vincent's childhood relationships before they barely started.

While skimming the pages detailing his friendship with Chris, Vincent paused at a certain passage. He looked at it with a growing sense of confusion and unease. This wasn't possible. Desperately trying to make sense of what he was looking at, Vincent reread the same few sentences over and over again.

I looked to my right to see the source of whoever interrupted my thoughts. My eyes fell upon a blond boy with a face dotted with freckles and acne. I immediately pegged him as an outcast who tried to befriend the new kid whenever possible since the new kid wasn't likely to have any other friends yet.

Vincent grabbed the manuscript that was put on the front seat of the car when he'd been at the book signing. He flipped through and crinkled his eyebrows when he found the paragraph in question. With the exception of changing from first person to third person, the paragraph in the manuscript was exactly like the paragraph in his journal. The same wording, the same punctuation—*the same exact sentences*. It was as if Kevin Larre had copied and pasted bits and pieces of his journals to create the manuscripts he was writing.

Vincent's face heated as the reality of his situation sunk in. Someone had broken into his home, his office, and his desk. Someone had broken into his life. Kevin Larre, whoever he was, had gotten his hands on his journals. There was no other explanation for it. Even if Vincent *did* believe in coincidences, this was just too unlikely not to have been done on purpose. Kevin Larre read his journals and put them word for word in his own work. He was bragging to Vincent that his secrets were no longer safe and hidden. He was making him look like a fool.

The thought of his journals in the hands of a stranger caused Vincent to pace frantically around his office. Nothing could be worse—nothing—than another person not only having access to his private memories, but actually using them to write and possibly publish for the world to read.

Vincent swaggered to his thermostat to lower the temperature in his office. It felt as if the room turned into a sauna within the past few minutes.

He turned around and pulled a handkerchief from his pocket to wipe the flow of sweat from his face. After a few swipes and some deep, labored breaths, Vincent managed to get his body under control. He tried to focus on a single object in the room to get his mind back on track and thinking clearly. He chose the lamp on the table next to his large leather chair. The lamp turned out to be a damaging focal point, however, because lying next to it was another yellow envelope.

He knew what it was and wished he were only imagining its presence. Walking slowly, as if approaching a bomb, Vincent came within reach of the table and gazed down at the envelope. He didn't even bother questioning the fact that it ended up in his office without him bringing it in himself. After realizing his journals had been looked at, he didn't find this too unbelievable.

The envelope had a picture of him and Lillian glued to the corner. He recognized it as the night they met at a club—Club Mayhem—when Vincent was in college. Not knowing what other choice he had, Vincent sat in the usually comfortable leather chair and opened the envelope to read the next chapter of his life.

ELEVEN

Club Mayhem

Vincent opened his eyes and looked at the clock. Anger grew inside him when he realized it was barely three in the morning and he was being jolted awake by stomping feet and loud voices.

He removed his ear plugs which seemed to be useless at blocking out the noise pollution his roommate created every night with his buddies. Vincent asked them repeatedly to keep it quiet when they returned home from the club, but the alcohol they consumed always wiped out the smidgen of consideration they may have had for him.

Vincent sat on the edge of his bed placing his feet flat on the floor and let his eyes adjust to the darkness. Without realizing it, Vincent fell asleep sitting in this position. It was the slamming of the fridge and beer bottles clanging together that again woke Vincent from his temporary nap. After hours of studying for his exam that was scheduled to begin in five hours, Vincent was exhausted. Being able to keep his scholarships depended on keeping up his grades. He refused to let the others in the room keep him awake.

His bare feet slapped loudly against the cool linoleum floor as he left his bedroom. Vincent sighed when his entrance to the kitchen wasn't as loud and intrusive as he intended.

Nothing could ever prepare Vincent for the scenes his roommate created with his friends after a night of drinking. John was currently leaning through the cutout in the wall that connected the kitchen to the modest eating nook. His feet were in the air and his head was in the sink as he drank water directly from the faucet.

"Water tastes good when it hits my tongue," he announced as he removed his lips from around the spigot. His words came out in a bit of a slur, alluding to the amount of alcohol he'd already consumed that night. If Vincent knew anything about his roommate, the drinking was not over. He made a mental note to clean everything in the kitchen with bleach, especially the faucet.

"Water tastes good when it doesn't hit your tongue, too," replied Alex, John's friend, as he giggled idiotically.

"Oh yeah?" continued John with his head still partly in the sink. The water now ran over the right side of his face, but he didn't seem to notice. "How would you know? Did you ever taste water without it hitting your tongue? Do you have some magical tongue that disappears when you tell it to?"

"That depends on who I'm with," Alex replied rolling his tongue over his lips multiple times, leaving them thoroughly moist.

"That's disgusting," Vincent chimed in.

"Vincent! You're up!" John exclaimed. "Alex, no more sexual innuendos. Vincent's virgin ears can't handle it."

Vincent ignored the comment. "Do you realize how loud you're being?"

"How was your exam?" John crawled through the wall and onto the counter, nearly falling into the sink. He barely missed landing on the sharp knives that were pointed up in the dish drainer.

Vincent's answer came with a roll of his eyes. "I'll let you know after I take it in five hours."

"Five hours? Dude, you should get some sleep."

"Thanks for the advice, Alex." Alex gave him a lopsided thumbs up before stumbling to the couch.

"What class is the exam in?" asked John.

"History of Russian Literature."

John leaned over like he was about to vomit. "Ugh, that sounds awful!"

"No it doesn't. Isn't Russian literature usually full of drunk people huddled in the snow?"

Vincent glanced at the girl who made the moronic comment. She came staggering out of the bathroom, clearly as drunk as the guys. He made no comment when another girl followed her out of the bathroom.

"Yeah," said Alex from his spot on the couch. "Everyone's always drinking vodka in Russia. I'd love it there if it wasn't so cold."

"You say that like you've been to Russia," said Vincent.

"Yeah, seriously dude. And besides, we got plenty of vodka here in America," John responded. "Observe." John tripped his way over to the fridge. Opening the freezer, he pulled out an unopened bottle of some slightly better than second-rate vodka.

"Haven't you had enough to drink tonight?" asked Vincent as he pulled the bottle out of his roommate's hands.

"Dude, I swear, I am drunk as a stump."

Vincent returned the bottle to the freezer. "I think you mean drunk as a skunk."

"No. I mean just what I said. I mean, just how drunk does a skunk ever get?"

"Probably drunker than a stump could."

"Touché," John said tapping his chin.

Vincent looked into John's slightly pink and glossed over eyes. There was obviously no comprehension taking place in that brain of his.

Giving up, Vincent returned to his room. "Try and keep it down, will you? Some of us actually have to work to stay in school."

It certainly wasn't easy for Vincent to get into Princeton. He knew he had the brains to get in, but money was a different story. A 1570 on his SATs along with a four point grade-point average was enough to get him a couple scholarships. However, he still had to take out loan after loan to cover the rest of the tuition and board. There was no way he could rely on his mother to help him with anything.

Vincent couldn't stand people like his roommate whose parents paid for what they couldn't achieve on their own academically. John's path to Princeton relied heavily on his doctor parents' deep pockets. There was no way Vincent would ever let his children get anything they didn't earn themselves.

He knew he would be successful once he graduated college. He planned to become a full-time writer, and while that may be a pipe dream for most, he was confident he would be instantly recognized as a great author.

Vincent would never have been able to get into Princeton without having the level of intelligence that he so obviously possessed. He worked hard to get where he was today. After coming this far, Vincent knew he couldn't go back to the situation he grew up in. Always moving, never having any stability. It wasn't his fault. He didn't have much choice who his mother was. He had been stuck with Janet Kraver whether he liked it or not. And most times, he definitely did not like it.

After he graduated and became successful, Vincent would be able to finally bid farewell to life with his mother. If he was ever going to get away from her, he needed to be a success once he graduated college. He *had* to be successful. He *would* be successful. There was no question about that.

He was already halfway through his first novel. Aiming to complete it by the time he graduated, it would launch him into the world of best sellers and book signings. Of course, in order to graduate, he would need to keep his scholarships by passing all his classes. That meant doing well on his exams which John made rather difficult when he stumbled into the apartment in the middle of the night.

History of Russian Literature was much different from the Idiot 101 classes that John took. Vincent was reading the works of great writers like Aleksandr Pushkin and Nikolay Gogol; Count Lev Tolstoy and Anton Chekov. He was

recognizing the nuances of literature that made any kind of writing something that would gain the recognition of intellectuals. That's who he would write for—intellectuals. Thoughts of future success and prestige put Vincent in a better mood as he crawled back into bed.

"Dude, I really need to dust off my eyes!"

Plugging his ears back up, Vincent laid his head on the pillow and hoped the drunk comments would cease for the night.

"Why are you a literature major? It seems like such a waste unless you're going to teach it."

John stood in the kitchen eating a bowl of cereal at two in the afternoon. It was his breakfast after waking up only thirty minutes ago.

"I told you before, I want to be a writer," Vincent answered.

"Then shouldn't you be a writing major?"

"I already know how to write. The only way to improve upon my writing is to read works of other successful writers. I don't need to learn about technique or plot or anything like that."

"I wish I had your confidence, man," said John. "Although sometimes I feel bad for you."

"What do you mean?" Vincent asked as he pulled a notebook out of his backpack.

"You focus so much on school and work that you don't seem to have any fun."

"Writing is fun for me." Vincent opened up to a blank page of his notebook and began scribbling notes.

"What's that?" asked John.

"My journal. I'm writing down some of the things you said last night."

John laughed. "You consider my drunk ramblings worth writing down?"

"Well," explained Vincent, "I may someday create an idiot character who says useless crap and makes a fool of himself just by opening his mouth."

"Sweet," said John looking genuinely pleased with himself.

The next few minutes were silent with the exception of John crunching his Apple Jacks. Vincent found it fascinating how much could be observed from simply sitting still for a few moments.

"You should definitely come to the club with us next time," John said.

Vincent answered without looking up. "I really don't have the time. I need to focus. It's harder than it looks to keep scholarships."

"But, imagine the material you could come up with by being at a club. If you think the shit I say when I come back is worth writing, you won't believe what you'll hear at the bar, or on the dance floor. It'll be like the Shakespeare of inebriation."

Putting his pen down, Vincent thought about John's suggestion. As much as he hated to admit it, his roommate made an excellent point. Going to a club would provide a plethora of characters for Vincent to store away for future work.

After a few seconds, he responded, "Okay, but as long as it's a Friday night. I don't want to go out during the week."

"Excellent night selection, bro," exclaimed an overly excited John. "Trust me, Friday night brings out the freakiest of the freaky."

"Great," said Vincent, obviously less enthusiastic than John.

Ignoring Vincent's bland response, John continued rambling. "I gotta call Alex and let him know. He won't wanna miss this. Vincent Kraver actually going out and having…dare I say it…fun!"

As John threw his cereal bowl in the sink and ran to his room, Vincent continued to write in his journal. John would definitely be making an appearance in his novel.

The guy staring back at Vincent in the bathroom mirror was nothing like the person he was used to seeing. Baggy jeans, a yellow button down shirt with vertical red stripes and a green backwards cap—who would own this stuff?

"I guess that would be John," Vincent muttered to himself, taking off the hat. He had to borrow John's clothes since his own wardrobe didn't produce anything appropriate for the club.

"I feel like a shmuck," Vincent said when John passed the bathroom door.

"You are a shmuck," John responded. "Ready to go?"

"Yeah, let's get this over with."

He stepped out of the bathroom and noticed Alex and John giving him strange looks.

"What," Vincent asked, touching his hair.

A sarcastic look came over John's face. "Alex, what's wrong with this picture?"

"Well, John," answered Alex, playing along, "after a brief glance, I'd say the pants are good, the shirt is bitchin',

and the hair is, well, ok. The thing that throws me, however, is that notebook in his hand."

"Ding! Ding! Ding!" John snatched the notebook from Vincent. "This stays home. I can't believe you think we would let you bring any kind of work with you to the club."

"But, you said it would be a good place to come up with characters. How am I supposed to remember everything?"

"Trust me," said Alex. "This night will be well documented." Before Vincent could protest, Alex held up a camera and snapped the first picture of the night.

John tossed the notebook onto Vincent's bed before pushing him toward the door. "Alright, here we go."

"Where are we going anyway?" asked Vincent.

"Club Mayhem," John and Alex responded.

"Club Mayhem?"

Vincent got nervous when the boys responded with mischievous grins.

An hour later, Vincent sat at a bar in a club that completely lived up to its name. He couldn't move an inch without bumping into another patron. The women all looked the same. Jeans that looked painted on, blouses that barely

covered mountainous breasts, and heels that made them all four or five inches taller.

Unfortunately, the men weren't any better. They wore jeans that emphasized every bulge and sported more jewelry than most of the women.

"Can I get you anything?" Vincent looked up and saw the bartender staring down at him.

"I'll have a beer."

"What kind?"

"I don't care."

The bartender placed a bottle in front of him. "Twelve dollars."

Vincent looked up again, this time confused. "Twelve dollars? For a beer?"

"You said you didn't care what kind."

"Jerk," Vincent muttered under his breath as the bartender walked away.

"It's a real rip off, isn't it?"

Before the bottle reached his lips, Vincent looked toward the source of the voice. He was dazzled by the mass of curly hair surrounding a beautiful face. Even in the darkness of the club, he could see the young woman had striking green

eyes that stood out with her pale skin, slightly reddened by rouge and alcohol.

"Yeah, well, I hardly ever go out, so I guess I can splurge on my drinks tonight."

"Maybe, I'll buy your next one. Drinks are cheaper for girls. Especially pretty ones." She smiled, showing a sparkling set of teeth. Vincent agreed she was pretty and liked the fact that she could admit it about herself.

"Is that right? I'll have to keep you with me all night then."

"Hey, just cause I'm pretty doesn't mean I'm easy."

"My apologies. I'm not used to clubs, so sorry if I seem awkward."

"You don't go out much? What do you usually do on Friday nights?"

Vincent took a sip of his overpriced beer before easing into the conversation. He enjoyed watching the petite woman hop onto the seat next to his.

"I spend most of my time writing. I'm in the middle of a novel."

"Ooh, that's interesting. What's it about?"

"Sorry, but that's something I will never divulge. At least until it's published, of course."

The woman raised one eyebrow. "You're a very confident person, aren't you?"

"I have to be to get anywhere in life."

"You must have strict parents."

Vincent chuckled at her far less than accurate assumption. Her puzzled look made her quite endearing. "My father left before I was born and my mother is somewhat of a nutcase."

"How so?"

"Well, she aspires to be great, but she can't figure out what she aspires to be great at."

The woman looked sorry. "That probably gets frustrating."

An awkward silence passed before Vincent managed to shift the conversation away from his mother. "Speaking of aspirations, what are yours?"

Sitting up in her seat, the woman looked eager to talk about herself. "I actually graduated from culinary school a year ago. I'm a sous chef at a local restaurant. Someday, I hope to run my own kitchen."

With each passing second, Vincent found himself growing more and more attracted to the young woman. He had never considered a relationship with anyone before, but

his mind was quickly changing. After all, this woman was beautiful, smart, ambitious, centered—basically, the polar opposite of his mother.

"Maybe, you can make me dinner someday and prove your talent as a chef."

"I'd love to. Anything you like in particular?"

"As long as there aren't any peanuts. My mom almost killed me a couple times when I was younger."

"Really?" she responded. "That's good to know in case you ever piss me off." She winked as she took a sip of her tall pink drink.

Vincent laughed at her dark sense of humor. "I'm Vincent by the way."

"Lillian," she replied, holding out her hand. Vincent shook it and noticed how soft her palms were. They sat smiling at each other until they were interrupted by a bright flash.

"Vincent Kraver meets a girl," shouted Alex still aiming the camera. "Never thought I'd see the day."

Vincent scowled at Alex even though he silently agreed.

TWELVE

Someone knew his past. Someone knew his secrets. That someone was Kevin Larre, but Vincent had no way of knowing who Kevin Larre was.

As he used his free hand to grab the phone on the table next to him, his gaze never left the manuscript which he held onto tightly, either out of fear or frustration. He couldn't think of anything else to do besides call Devon.

"Hey, it's Vincent," he said, barely giving Devon time to say hello. "Did you find any information on Kevin Larre?"

"No," his agent replied. "I called around to other agencies and publishing houses in case he never went through an agent. No one's ever heard of him. He must be brand new."

Vincent was silent as he tried to think of some other way to identify the mystery author.

"Vincent?"

"Yeah, Dev, I'm still here. I'm just confused. How can we not figure this out?"

Vincent knew he sounded nervous. There was no way to disguise his voice like everything was fine.

"Why are you letting him get to you? You're a great author and apparently he's no one." Vincent was relieved that the concern in Devon's voice sounded sincere. At least he thought it did. He wasn't really sure what to think about anything anymore.

"It's getting more complicated, Devon," Vincent replied hesitantly.

"How so?" Devon asked. "Did you get any other manuscripts from him?"

"Yeah, three more, all about me. Private things about me that…that…I just don't know how he got this information." That was a lie, of course. Kevin Larre read his journals. He broke into his life uninvited and threw his stolen knowledge back in Vincent's face. "This is the last one though."

"How do you know?"

"Just a feeling." That was another lie. Vincent was positive he wouldn't receive any more manuscripts. The last journal entry was from the night after he met Lillian. After that, he focused more on finishing his first novel and courting his future wife and neglected his journals. There was nothing left for Kevin Larre to write about.

Devon's concern seemed to grow more. It wasn't often that Vincent Kraver couldn't explain something, and even rarer that he could barely finish his sentences. "Have you considered calling the police? Maybe they could issue a restraining order."

"How's that possible if we don't know who Kevin Larre is?" asked Vincent.

"That's true," Devon replied. "But, maybe they can help figure out who this guy is."

Vincent thought about his agent's suggestion before responding. "No. I don't think that's necessary. Besides, I don't want to alarm my family and worry them over something that's probably nothing."

"Well, that's your decision," said Devon. "Think about it, though. I'll keep searching for information. I'll call if I come up with anything."

"Thanks." Vincent hung up once again without any knowledge of Kevin Larre's true identity. Still gripping the manuscript, Vincent walked over to his desk. He threw the chapter down on his keyboard and watched the paper slowly unwrinkle itself. The sound of the crackling paper was magnified by the thick silence that filled the rest of the office.

Devon's suggestion to call the police made perfect sense at this point in time. Kevin Larre had broken into his car and into his home. He posed as a direct threat to him and his family. Vincent was concerned with his family's safety, but something deep down still kept him from taking his concerns to the authorities.

He could not voice his reasons to Devon because he knew his agent would never understand. After all, Devon would never realize the success that Vincent had gained. Devon lacked the talent and the creativity—not the best combination for someone who wanted to write bestsellers. Since he'd never be as successful as Vincent, he couldn't possibly understand Vincent's point of view.

Vincent also knew his reason would sound a little selfish. To everyone—not just Devon. As disturbing as the chapters were, he was enjoying the fact that someone admired him enough to write a biography. He was also somewhat flattered that his writing could inspire someone on such a profound level, even if that someone was a bit on the stalker side. Vincent Kraver was an amazing writer who made ordinary people do extraordinary things. Now that he really thought about it, maybe his reasons for not reporting Kevin Larre were more than a *little* selfish.

There was another major thing keeping him from voicing his concerns to the police and his family. Vincent had a growing suspicion that someone close to him was writing the manuscripts. The only ones who knew of his journals were Lillian and Patrick. He wasn't sure of how they could have broken into his desk or office though. He was the only one who knew where the spare keys were. At least he thought he was the only one who knew until he was proven very wrong.

He also tried to think about who knew he'd be at the book signing today. Devon knew, of course, but there was no way he was intelligent enough to hide such a big secret as being Kevin Larre from Vincent. If anything, he would have bragged about it after Vincent initially complimented his work.

Lillian was also aware of his book signing, but she was at the restaurant all day. He was pretty sure of that. His wife was an excellent chef and the restaurant would fall apart without her.

The strongest reason for not reporting Kevin Larre was probably the most selfish of all. Vincent Kraver was the author of fifteen mystery crime novels. He loved the thrill of a mystery, the suspense, the danger. Reporting Kevin Larre would end the delivery of the manuscripts and the mystery being created. Vincent craved mystery, and Kevin Larre was the only person in his life giving it to him.

But, what was he thinking? There would be no more deliveries anyway. Now that the journal entries stopped, wouldn't the manuscripts?

The grating sound of the phone interrupted Vincent's thoughts. He ran to answer it hoping Devon finally uncovered some useful information.

"Hey, Dev. What did you find out?"

"You're not even writing a book now and you're still letting work dominate your life."

Vincent's head rolled backwards on his neck when he heard the irate tone in Lillian's voice. "Why are you so angry? I still have work obligations when I'm not writing."

"What about your family obligations?"

“What are you talking about?”

“Remember Neil? Your son? He’s in a cab on his way home from school right now because you forgot to pick him up.” Vincent looked at the grandfather clock that stood in the corner of his office and was shocked to see it was after five.

“Shit. I’m sorry. I’ve had a really hectic day and I just forgot.”

“Don’t apologize to me. It’s Neil you should be worried about,” Lillian said. “I’ve never heard him so angry.”

“I’m sure he’ll understand once I explain what I’ve been through today.”

“I hope he does for your sake,” Lillian continued. “I just thought I’d give you some fair warning.”

“Thanks for the heads up,” Vincent said. He paused to give Lillian a chance to ask him what had happened to him that day. He realized he’d be waiting a long time for his wife to care enough about his day. “Well, I guess I’ll see you when you get home from work. Probably around midnight?”

“I don’t know. I may grab some drinks with Franci. Things have been hectic around here lately.”

“Out for drinks? Aren’t you a little old to be going out for drinks after midnight?”

“You just get meaner and meaner every day.”

"I'm sorry," Vincent answered. "But, there aren't many women with jobs and families who choose to go out drinking that late. Especially during the week."

"Don't bother waiting up for me." Lillian hung up before he could respond. Yet another fight to add to their growing list.

Vincent didn't understand why she was getting so upset over his comments. Didn't he have a valid reason to be concerned that his wife, a woman in her mid-fifties, still frequented bars to unwind after a long day of cooking? Vincent always thought cooking was supposed to be a relaxing experience—especially for women.

His thoughts were interrupted when he heard a car door slam in front of the house. He walked out of his office to face the wrath of his son.

Vincent made his way into the foyer just as the front door swung open. To his surprise, Justin came waltzing in with no sign of Neil following him.

"Where's Neil?" Vincent asked his son's friend before letting him go up the stairs.

"He's paying the cab driver," Justin said. "He can't wait to talk to you." The look on Justin's face told Vincent he was looking forward to what Neil had to say.

"How about you go up to Neil's room while I talk to him?"

"I can't stay and watch?"

"Either go upstairs or get that cab to take you home right now."

"Okay, okay. Just trying to be social." Justin hopped up the stairs and shut the door to Neil's room. At least Vincent and Neil would have some privacy to talk. He didn't want to have to bring him to his office.

However, when Neil finally came through the front door, Vincent thought it would have been a good idea to have Justin around as a witness. His son certainly looked very upset.

"Neil, I'm so sorry I forgot to pick you up. If you'd just let me explain…"

"I don't want to listen to your excuses," Neil said, cutting him off. "You shouldn't have to make up reasons for forgetting your own kid."

"I didn't forget. I just got distracted."

"With what? Work? Your book signing? Yeah, I can see how a book signing can distract you. You sit there for hours signing your name for people like you're the king of the universe, and then your forget about the little people like your son."

"It's more complicated than that."

"I even gave you my car to use. How could you forget about me when you were driving *my* car all day?"

"I've had a lot to deal with all day." Vincent was starting to get sick of defending himself. "And, I get paid for book signings and for writing. Everything I do is for you and Susan. I'm giving you the opportunity to become what you want and you never act grateful for anything."

Neil made a face that showed his disbelief in what Vincent just said. "Are you kidding? You don't do anything for me and Susan. You do everything for Vincent Kraver. You try and make your own kids look good to make yourself look good. You care about yourself and no one else. Anyone who thinks otherwise is blind."

"I give you everything I didn't have growing up."

"You're blinded by your self-righteousness."

That statement took Vincent aback. "What's that supposed to mean?"

"You're convinced everything you do is right and good. You think people love you and think you're great. You're self-centered, just like your mother."

If there was anything anyone could say to knock the wind out of Vincent, it was Neil's last comment. He took a step toward Neil and tried to keep his voice steady. "I will never be like my mother. *Never*."

Neil laughed as he climbed the stairs to his bedroom. "Please. You already are your mother. You're just too ashamed to admit it." And with that, he slammed his door and left Vincent standing at the bottom of the steps in complete misery.

There was no way Neil was right. Vincent tried so hard to avoid becoming his mother. Nothing scared him more. Not even the idea of having a stalker who broke into his car, his house and his past scared Vincent more than the idea of turning into Janet Kraver.

The more he thought about it, the more nervous he became. He had to make sure Neil's comment would never become a fact. Not knowing what else to do or where else to go, Vincent went to find answers to the questions that plagued him, thanks to his son's rant.

Grabbing his coat, he took the liberty of borrowing Neil's car again, not bothering to ask for his son's permission. It's not like the little brat paid for it himself. It killed Vincent to know that everything he did for his family went unappreciated.

He jumped in the car and drove to the one place that might somehow ease his troubled mind.

THIRTEEN

The smell of Everly made Vincent gag the instant he entered the building. He passed the receptionist who offered him a tired smile despite probably being miserable. How could anyone willingly come to work in such a place everyday and be happy?

Vincent was about to turn the corner when the receptionist called to him. “Sir, you have to sign in.” As ridiculous as he found it to sign in to an assisted living facility, he complied. He signed his name and wrote the name of who he was visiting.

“Ah, Ms. Kraver. She’s a favorite around here.”

Vincent shook his head at what he assumed was a false statement she told every visitor to Everly. After looking at the sign-in book, however, the number of visitors was extremely low. “You don’t have to lie. I know my mother and favorite is not a word I’d use to describe her.”

The receptionist looked confused. “No, really, she’s a joy to be around. She has such fascinating stories about her life.”

“Most of them are made up.”

“If that’s true, it’s no wonder you’re such a successful writer. Your mother is creative. You must take after her.” She smiled one more time before flipping through an open magazine on the desk. Vincent’s jaw clenched. He hated being compared to his mother. The fact that it happened twice in one day added to his mounting frustration.

The walk down the hallway to his mother's room was nothing short of depressing. The residents of Everly all looked eerily similar. The few who still had some hair didn't bother to do any styling. *It's not like I'm one to talk*, Vincent thought as he swept his hand over his balding dome. Their eyes all looked lost and distant. Many just stared straight ahead in their wheelchairs while focusing intently on the air in front of them.

As Vincent passed some of the patients, a few smiled, happy to see a younger face in their elderly establishment. Most of them were constantly chewing, although Vincent couldn't imagine what they'd be chewing on. The odds were low that any of them housed teeth in their wrinkled mouths.

A couple of women, probably in their eighties, sat in a lounge deep in conversation--at least one of them was. The other focused on the small television and didn't hear a word her friend was saying. Vincent wondered if that was truly the case or if the woman used her old age as an excuse for not listening to people. One of the advantages of growing old was certainly the easier use of selective hearing.

Vincent looked behind him when he heard a motor quickly approaching. Managing to step aside just in time to avoid becoming Everly road kill, he cursed at the old speed demon who didn't seem to notice his surroundings. He looked around to see if anyone else heard him curse, but luckily it seemed like everyone had the volume of their hearing aids turned down.

Vincent finally came to a door with a sign that said "Kraver" on the outside. He knocked before entering, more for his convenience than for his mother's. The last time he showed up unannounced, he got a full frontal view of Janet in her birthday suit. That was definitely not an easy thing to recover from.

"Hey, mom."

"Vincent!" Janet Kraver sat in a chair next to her bed with a standing mirror on the table next to her. "I thought you may have forgotten about me."

"You're kind of hard to forget," Vincent replied.

Janet didn't bother getting up to greet her son. She looked comfortable in her floral nightgown and pink slippers. The part of her outfit that confused Vincent, however, was the huge sunglasses that covered half her face.

Janet turned her attention to her mirror and looked at herself without any form of expression. After watching his mother for a few seconds, Vincent finally gave up.

"What exactly are you doing?" he asked.

"Practicing."

"Practicing what?"

"My bingo face."

"What do you mean? What's a bingo face?"

"The face I put on when I play bingo."

"I didn't know you needed a face to play bingo."

"You don't if you're an amateur. But I'm a professional bingo player." Janet pointed to her eyes. "See these sunglasses? They prevent my opponents from seeing my eyes. That way they won't know what I'm thinking."

Realizing this must be his mother's new life dream, Vincent decided to play along. At least she wasn't hurting anyone. "I didn't know bingo was a professional game."

"Oh yes," answered Janet excitedly. "It's a highly technical process that involves a great deal of skill and intuition. I see them play it on the television, and the really good ones all wear dark sunglasses."

Vincent didn't think it was necessary to explain that the game she saw on television was poker, not bingo. What would be the point of telling her? She would just end up accusing him of ruining another one of her dreams.

"So I'm guessing you play a lot of bingo while you're here, huh?"

"There's not much else to do when you get no visitors." Janet removed her sunglasses to show Vincent she was glaring at him.

"You bring this up every time I come visit," Vincent said, returning his mother's glare. "Maybe I'd visit more often if you'd stop chastising me all the time."

"I can't believe you treat your mother like this, after all she went through to raise you."

"I also wish we could get through a whole visit without you referring to yourself in the third person."

"You've never been grateful for anything I've done for you. I gave you life, but you probably criticize me for that."

Vincent was tired of arguing with everyone he talked to today and tried desperately to change the topic. "Do you ever win anything when you play bingo?"

"As a matter of fact, I win every night," she replied happily, placing the sunglasses back on and forgetting she was angry at him.

"Good for you. How much do you win?"

"It varies. Tonight I walked away with the grand prize. Thirteen dollars!"

"Wow," said Vincent trying his best to feign enthusiasm. "That's great. It sounds like you finally found your calling."

"I'd say so," Janet replied.

Vincent sat with his mother for a few more minutes chatting over useless topics. He then decided he'd devoted enough time to his mother and stood up.

"I think I need to head out. I had a busy day signing books and stuff."

"Signing books makes you tired? You're getting lazy like your father."

"Bye, mom."

"Bye, Vincent."

Vincent smiled as he turned to leave. He was relieved his mother compared him to his father instead of to her. He wasn't sure if he'd be able to handle hearing that comment three times in one day.

He turned to observe his mother one last time before leaving. Janet was staring at her reflection, unmoving, perfecting her bingo face. He silently wished her all the luck in the world before leaving.

The journey back down the hall was no less depressing than before. Not much ever happened at Everly.

Vincent was more convinced than ever after his visit that he was nothing like his mother. It hadn't taken him seventy-five years to find his purpose in life. And, he'd certainly amounted to more than having a good bingo face.

No. There was no way Vincent Kraver was *anything* like Janet Kraver.

Vincent walked quickly past the receptionist on his way out. She glanced up from her magazine just as he was heading out the door.

"Mr. Kraver, this came for you."

Vincent spun around and saw her holding out a yellow envelope. He stared at it for a few seconds as if not recognizing what it was.

"Mr. Kraver?"

"When did this get here?" he asked.

"About ten minutes ago. You were visiting with your mother and he didn't want to disturb you."

"Who? Did he give a name?"

The receptionist looked confused. "No. He just told me to give this to you."

"What did he look like?"

"Dark shaggy hair, black clothes. He had sunglasses. Kind of weird for the evening." She continued to hold out the envelope. "Is everything okay?"

Okay? No, everything is not okay. What could possibly be in that envelope? I stopped writing in my journals after I met

Lillian. There is no other information for Kevin Larre to discover. There should be no more manuscripts!

"Everything's fine," he said, finally taking the envelope. "Thank you." He headed out the door and glanced briefly at the picture glued to the corner—Susan at a party surrounded by boys. Lots and lots of boys.

FOURTEEN

Daddy's Little Girl

Vincent's life had been getting increasingly hectic. The arguments with his wife were becoming more and more regular. He tried to push his son to focus more on getting into an Ivy League school. But, a stranger began to take away any sanity that he may have retained after dealing with his family issues. Vincent always found his role as a writer a great way to take control of a life that he sometimes found hard to handle.

The greatest accomplishment for Vincent had been being able to finally take control of his life. Growing up, he'd been unable to enjoy life because he'd been forced to live in many horrible situations. Vincent had to go where Janet Kraver went. He had to live with the men his mother thought she loved. And, he had to watch as these men eventually used his mother, abused her both physically and emotionally, and then kicked them out. Finally, after graduating college, marrying Lillian, having children, and completing his fifteenth novel, Vincent felt he was the author of his own life. He felt he was in control, and no one other than himself would write his future.

Now there was a man—a mystery man—taking away that one stable role in his life.

With every person he knew seeming to be an object of opposition to the life he thought he had, Vincent found himself reevaluating everyone. His relationship with Lillian was clearly on the rocks. Neil always acted like he was the worst father on the face of the earth even though Vincent knew he gave his son everything a well brought-up child should get. There was nothing he didn't give to his children. He was certainly a vast improvement from Janet Kraver.

Susan was the only one in his life that Vincent didn't have any issues with. She got upset with him for bringing up her weight gain, but sometimes it was the parent's duty to bring up the hard topics with children, even if that topic was guaranteed to cause turbulence.

Vincent was concerned about his daughter. He saw her becoming like every other overweight child in America. He was confused because she went to track practice every day after school. If anything, Susan should be in great shape. She did cross country in the fall, indoor track in the winter, and track and field in the spring. Why, then, did she look like she put on more and more weight over the past couple years?

His questions about Susan made Vincent wonder exactly what his daughter did every day after school. She claimed she had track practice, but doubt began to nag at him. How well did he really know Susan? Was it possible she was

lying about her after school activities? Was there a lot about Susan that Vincent didn't have a clue about?

"Bye, Susan." Susan turned to look at Justin as he waved to her flirtatiously. She couldn't wait until she got her license and didn't have to carpool with Neil and his jackass friend to school every day.

Plastering on her cheesiest smile, she waved back and wished him luck on his calculus exam that she knew he'd fail. "Neil has such idiot friends," she thought.

Susan walked into homeroom and took her seat by the window. She avoided eye contact with as many people as possible. Most of the girls in her class hated her. Their jealousy pissed her off. It wasn't her fault she was able to make it with their boyfriends while they were too uncomfortable to take their tops off. What was the point of having a boyfriend if you weren't going to give him what he wanted? Susan knew what guys wanted, and she was glad she could give it to them.

It was all Susan wanted in life—to be able to please men. It was upsetting that she had to go to such lengths to get male approval, but it's not like she would ever get it at home. Her father was always busy with his writing. She was the last thing on Vincent Kraver's mind, especially when he went to

book signings every week. No, when it came to male approval, her father was the last person Susan could turn to.

Neil, of course, wasn't any better. Her brother did all he could to keep her at a distance. She couldn't go to him for advice, comfort, or even a casual conversation. The door to his room was constantly closed to her and everyone else in the house. Susan didn't understand how she ended up with a father and a brother who seemed to care so little about her.

Without anyone else to turn to, she settled for the boys in her school. Susan craved the attention, almost to the point of a sickness. She couldn't help herself. Boys made her feel desirable. They made her feel like she was worth having around. And, that felt good.

So, she gave the boys what she knew they wanted. Unfortunately, that meant most of the girls despised her. She was accused of being the cause of most of the breakups in her school.

That isn't to say she didn't have any girlfriends. Her best friend, Lauren, loved to hear about Susan's "sexcapades" with the guys in their grade. She especially loved it when Susan hooked up with Eric Riller, boyfriend of Tara Lamberg, the head cheerleader and most stuck-up girl in school. Susan and Lauren managed to snag dates to the senior prom when they were in eighth grade. Tara's face when Susan came out of the elevator with Eric after disappearing upstairs for an hour

was priceless. Lauren made sure to snap a picture of Susan with Eric, as well as with every other guy she ever hooked up with.

The bell rang dismissing the students from homeroom, and Susan moved through the overcrowded hallways trying her best to avoid knocking into everyone. This was a nearly impossible feat for anyone who went to Morris High. After turning several corners, Susan made her way into the locker room. She cursed her own damn, bad luck that she ended up with first period gym. It was especially horrible in the winter when the locker room felt colder than the temperature outside.

"Hey, bitch."

"Hey, skank."

Lauren and Susan greeted each other the same way every morning. At least, Lauren got stuck with the same first period schedule.

"How was your night last night?" Lauren asked.

"Pretty boring. I went to Tom's house for an hour or so, but nothing exciting happened."

"Maybe it would have been better if I was there."

"Of course, everything is better when you're there," Susan replied. "But, you had to be at the flower shop."

"Dude, my mom got me the job. I can't just not go."

"You can't lie? Seriously, you need to focus more on yourself."

Susan put her backpack down on the bench and took out a bottle of water. She popped a pill in her mouth and swallowed it with one swig of water. Lauren watched with a tinge of jealousy.

"I wish I could swallow pills like you. I can never go on any kind of medication that involves swallowing a pill."

"What's the big deal?" Susan asked.

"I don't know what it is. I always choke on pills."

Susan shrugged her shoulders. "I don't really have a choice. If I didn't take it every day, I'd have to rely on guys using condoms. And, high school boys can't usually be trusted with that kind of thing."

Susan and Lauren dressed for gym in silence as more girls trudged into the locker room. No one was a fan of having to change this early in the day.

The gym was almost as cold as the locker room, and rows of students sat on the floor with their arms wrapped around themselves trying to keep warm and stay awake while the gym teachers took attendance. Susan sat in the third row in between Jimmy and Luke. Jimmy smiled half-heartedly at her, probably wanting to skip class and sleep in his car. He

had a nice car. Susan would know since she'd seen the back seat several times.

Luke was another story. Susan never saw him outside of school. She sometimes wondered if he had any social life. She went to a lot of parties, and Luke never showed up at any of them. However, she had to keep in mind that there were over three hundred students in her class alone, so the chances of Susan seeing everyone at the parties she attended were slim.

"Okay, let's get started," said the gym teacher without much enthusiasm. Susan thought there should be a law against having physical education so early in the day. There was a chorus of grumbles as the students stood up from the cold gym floor. "Alright. Ten jumping jacks. Ready, begin. One, two, three..."

The rest of first period gym was filled with half sit-ups, sleepy push-ups, and an extremely unexciting game of volleyball. After twenty minutes of pretending to get exercise, most students broke off into tiny groups to have their own conversations. The gym teachers were usually too busy focusing on drills for their teams' after-school practices to discipline anyone.

Susan looked at her teacher, Mrs. Booker, and laughed. Mrs. Booker was the coach for the girls' track team, the after-school activity her parents assumed she went to everyday. She

sometimes wondered how her parents even remembered her name since they paid so little attention to her.

Her after school activities had nothing to do with running, though they were extremely physical. No, she could definitely never survive being on the track team. In fact, she was probably one of the worst runners ever. Back in sixth grade, after the weekly mile run in gym class, someone once asked her if she had asthma. Susan didn't have asthma, but running never came as an easy task for her. Every semester she would join the team long enough to appear in the yearbook photo in case her parents ever happened to see the pictures, but she would always quit as soon as possible.

The whistle finally blew telling the students they could return to the locker rooms to change. Susan waited for Lauren to make her way across the gym before going in to change.

"So, are you energized?" Lauren joked.

"Extremely. Can't you tell?" Susan liked that Lauren was just as sarcastic as her. It was probably what made their friendship so strong.

"What are you doing tonight?" Lauren asked as she slipped into her regular school clothes.

"Probably going to Sean's," Susan replied. "Did you wanna come?"

"Sean's again? Is he becoming your boyfriend?"

Susan smiled at her friend's slight cheekiness. "Yeah right. Since when is anyone my boyfriend?"

"That's true. He is really cute though. It probably wouldn't be so bad."

"I don't know any boys who want relationships. It's no fun for them if they actually have to care about the girls they're with."

"So, you prefer boys that don't care about you?"

"That's not what I said. The guys I hook up with care about me. They're just not forced to care. We have fun together and this makes everyone happy."

"Except for the guys' actual girlfriends," Lauren added pointing a finger at Susan.

Susan smiled and rolled her eyes. "That's not my concern."

"And, that's why girls hate you."

"All except you, right?"

"Oh, of course. You're my ho."

"If that were the case, I would make you the most successful pimp in Morristown."

A big grin spread across Lauren's face. "Now that is something to keep in mind."

"Will do," replied Susan. "But for tonight, I'm going to Sean's."

"And, your parents still think you're going to track practice?"

"Yep."

"No offense, Suze, but you're parents are extremely dense."

"Believe me, I take no offense. I don't think my parents would remember I exist if I didn't go home for dinner every Sunday night."

The bell ending first period finally rang, releasing them from the freezing locker room.

"I'll see you at lunch," Susan said as she and Lauren headed their separate ways down the hall.

"See ya, babe."

"So what is the craziest thing you've ever done?" Sean rubbed her shoulders gently as they faced each other on his bed. Susan liked it when boys caressed her gently. It made her feel like they cared about her comfort.

"Well, there was this one time when me and Lauren went skinny dipping in the school's pool on a dare."

Sean laughed, feeling completely relaxed with Susan. "I guess that is pretty crazy. Did you get caught?"

"I wish. The night security guard is really cute." Sean gave her a hurt look. "But, not as cute as you, of course," Susan continued.

"You're pretty cute too," Sean said, pulling her closer.

"Speaking of being cute together," Susan said as she reached into her purse, "I say we document our cute time together." She pulled a digital camera out of her bag and turned it on.

"Wow," said Sean. "I never would have imagined you to be so kinky to bring a camera to one of our after school sessions."

"There're a lot of things you don't know about me," she replied with a wink.

Susan sat above Sean and straddled him. She took a couple of pictures before handing him the camera.

"Now take a couple pictures of me," she said and smiled her sweetest smile. As Sean took pictures of the girl above him, Susan slowly began unsnapping the buttons of her shirt. She wore this shirt specially for Sean because he liked how he could rip it open with one tug. And Susan liked to please her boys any way she could.

Sean continued snapping photos as Susan's shirt fell to the floor and she was left wearing a pink bra with purple and red hearts. The clasp was located in the front of the bra, something she liked to tease Sean with, among others.

Putting the camera down on his nightstand, Sean looked at Susan with a serious look in his eyes. "You should be my girlfriend."

Totally taken by surprise, Susan stopped her little striptease. After a few seconds, she responded. "Look, Sean, we have so much fun together. Don't you think a relationship would complicate things?"

"I like you," Sean replied. "A lot. Don't you like me?"

"Of course I like you," Susan said leaning in close to kiss him.

"So, what do you say?"

"Can I say that I'll think about it?"

"You will? Really?"

Susan closed her eyes, hating to have to lie to Sean. "Yes, I'll think about it."

"Okay. You can think about it."

Susan decided it was best to let all conversation come to a close. The next couple of hours went by in a blur as she knew this would be her last time with Sean.

Susan walked straight to her bedroom like she did every night when she came home from "track practice." As usual, her mother wasn't home, her father was busy in his office, and Neil was listening to his stereo way too loudly.

She never felt more alone than when she was home. Kicking off her shoes, she booted up her laptop to upload the photos from her digital camera. She wished she didn't have to end things with Sean, but she knew men were never happy in relationships. It just wouldn't work.

She looked at the pictures of Sean and herself. They were the epitome of amateur nude shots, but she loved them. She turned on her printer and made hard copies of all the photos.

After they were done printing, Susan reached under her bed and removed a shoebox. Taking the top off, Susan placed the newly printed photos into the box with hundreds of other similar shots. Susan had been with many men, and Sean was merely another addition to her sprawling collection.

With a tinge of sadness, Susan replaced the lid of the shoebox, slid it back under the bed, fell back on a pillow, and picked up her phone to call Lauren.

FIFTEEN

Vincent laid awake in bed for hours. Sleep was impossible for him to come by after reading the latest delivery from Kevin Larre. What he read couldn't possibly be true. There was no way his daughter carried on like that slut in the manuscript.

It was alarming. However, much of what was written could make sense. After all, Vincent had noticed Susan's weight gain for several months now. If she was going to track practice every day after school, wouldn't she be in better shape than she appeared to be in?

No. Vincent would not believe what he read. The thought of Susan giving herself to so many boys made him sick. And the photographs...No child of his would ever do such a demeaning thing. Besides, Susan was only fourteen years old. How could a fourteen-year-old girl have sunk so low as to have herself photographed in such crude positions?

Vincent decided not to believe what Kevin Larre had written. It was the only way for him to keep any form of sanity. Kevin Larre was trying to ruin his life. After proving he was able to break into his past so easily, he was now trying to control his present. Well, Vincent would not let that happen. His life would remain his own, and he refused to give in to Kevin Larre's attempt to destroy him and his family.

Vincent closed his eyes and willed for sleep to come. His mind would still not let him stop wondering about Susan, however. What if it was true? What if Susan was looking for male companionship by sleeping with the boys in her school? What if she was taking pictures of what Kevin Larre so eloquently labeled as “sexcapades”?

He knew there was only one way to find out. Unfortunately, he would have to wait until morning to investigate the truth behind what was written in the manuscript. Vincent prayed that Kevin Larre’s latest chapter was pure fiction. Disturbing and horrifying fiction.

“Suze, are you ready to go?” Neil stood by the front door swinging his keys around the tip of his index finger.

“I’ll be down in a minute,” she called from upstairs. As usual, Susan was taking forever in the bathroom with her make-up.

“Are you trying to make yourself pretty for Justin?” Neil smiled because he knew how annoyed Susan got whenever his friend hit on her, which was often.

“Justin’s a prick,” she replied as she hopped down the steps.

Vincent walked into the foyer to say goodbye to his kids. He was somewhat relieved that Susan didn’t like Justin. At least if what he read last night was true, he wouldn't have to worry about finding his daughter with *that* jackass.

Neil looked at Vincent and didn't bother waiting for Susan to get to the bottom of the stairs. Instead, he headed out the front door to wait in his car. He was obviously still mad at Vincent for forgetting to pick up him up yesterday. Vincent wondered how long his grudge would last.

Susan went to the kitchen to grab her lunch before following Neil out the front.

"Have a nice day at school," Vincent said when she passed him.

Susan stopped short and looked at him. She looked confused that he was talking to her. "What?"

"I said have a good day at school," he repeated.

She waited a few seconds as if trying to comprehend another language. "Thanks," she replied slowly, and then she turned to meet Neil in his car. Vincent watched her and was upset that such a small interaction between them seemed to catch her off guard.

After the car disappeared, Vincent walked to the kitchen where Lillian was washing breakfast dishes. He stood watching her and wondering if she knew anything about Susan.

"Morning," he said.

"Morning," she replied without looking up.

"How was last night?"

Lillian's body stiffened, confusing Vincent. "What?"

"You went out with Franci for drinks, right?"

"Oh yeah," Lillian said as her body relaxed. "It was fine."

"Where'd you go?"

"Uh…Sorento's."

"That's a nice place."

"Yeah, they had some jazz there last night."

Vincent wondered why Lillian wasn't looking at him. She must be holding a grudge from yesterday just like Neil.

"Do you know when Susan's track meets are?" Lillian finally turned to face him. It was an odd question he just asked considering he never showed any interest in their kids' extracurricular activities.

"Um, I don't know," she said rubbing her head. "She never gave me her schedule."

"Why is that?" he asked.

"I'm usually busy at the restaurant. I wouldn't have time to go see her run."

"So how do you know she is actually on the track team?"

Lillian gave him a look like he was asking the most ridiculous questions. In a way, he was. "What else would she be staying after school for?"

Vincent wondered if he should bring up what he read in the manuscript. It would be a rather risky topic to mention to Lillian, who was already pissed at him for forgetting to pick up their son yesterday. As a matter of fact, it would be a risky topic to mention whether they were having a fight or not. How many mothers would react favorably to being told their daughters aren't actually running track but meeting up with boys for sexual rendezvous every day? That's not exactly an after-school activity that would be supported by many parents.

Vincent also knew that it would be a mistake to mention this to Lillian because he wasn't sure of its validity. He got the information from Kevin Larre, a person whom he never met and had never heard of until a few days ago. He was also someone who proved to be very sneaky and uncaring about Vincent's private life. Kevin Larre was a criminal, and there was no reason for Vincent to trust him.

However, there was still a chance that Kevin Larre delivered the truth in his writing. Thinking back over the manuscripts detailing Vincent's childhood, the events were described with cunning accuracy. It would be out of character for

Kevin Larre to all of a sudden write something that wasn't a direct reflection of the truth.

Vincent saw that Lillian was still staring at him, waiting for an answer. Even though he was positive Susan didn't exactly run track after school, he didn't want to mention the other disturbing possibility until he was sure it was true. He knew Lillian was waiting for a response, however, so he came up with one, although he knew it would make his wife even more angry at him.

"Well, Lil, you can't tell me you haven't been noticing Susan gaining weight lately."

Vincent almost felt like he should duck to avoid the daggers shooting from Lillian's eyes. "You've got to be kidding me," she retorted. Vincent expected Lillian to react unfavorably to talking about Susan's weight yet again, but after witnessing this reaction, Vincent wondered if it would have been a better idea to have just told her their daughter was an after-school sexaholic.

"Let me make my argument before you go off on a rant about me being a horrible father," Vincent said. Lillian folded her arms across her chest and leaned against the counter. Taking this as a silent go ahead, Vincent continued. "Susan claims to be running track every day after school. Running is a great exercise, especially when it comes to maintaining a healthy weight. However, it's obvious that Susan has been putting on weight at a regular pace. Now, isn't it a little weird that she's getting heavier even though she says she is running every day?" Vincent let out a deep breath, relieved that he could get through his side of the argument for once without being interrupted.

"Are you done?" Lillian asked, maintaining her stance at the counter.

"Yes."

Lillian stood still for a few minutes and looked like she was actually thinking about what he said. After some consideration, she finally spoke. "Okay. Just because Susan is on the track team does not mean she isn't going to gain any weight. Even if she exercises every day, it's still possible she is eating unhealthy, and maybe as her parents, we can start monitoring what she eats a bit more so that she isn't unhealthy. Would that make you feel better?"

Vincent didn't think he'd be able to talk to Lillian anymore without her anger toward him increasing. "Yeah," he said and started to walk out of the kitchen. Stopping at the door, Vincent remembered another part of the manuscript from the night before that he wanted to ask Lillian about.

He turned and faced his wife, unsure of how to prepare himself for the annoyance Lillian would certainly feel when he asked his blunt question.

"Lillian, is Susan on birth control?"

Dropping the bowl she was washing, Lillian turned to face Vincent with a look of disbelief. “What on earth does that have to do with anything?”

“It’s just something I’m wondering about.”

“Why?”

Vincent didn’t answer, not because he didn’t have a valid response, but because he hadn’t thought about a good way to answer her without telling her about the manuscript. How could he possibly explain to his wife why he expected their daughter of being on birth control?

“I think it’s a valid question for a father to ask. Susan is, after all, in high school and surrounded by boys.

Vincent wasn’t sure how much longer he could continue this conversation with Lillian without her throwing dishes at him. But he had to know about Susan, and he wasn’t going to stop asking questions until he got an answer, no matter how unsavory that answer may be.

Thankfully, Lillian didn’t make him ask anymore, and she managed to answer back without hurling anything at him. “Yes,” she said. “Susan has been on birth control for almost two years now.”

Vincent would have preferred a dish or two to the head. “When were you planning on telling me?”

"There was no reason to tell you. I didn't think you cared that much."

"What makes you think I wouldn't care? And what makes you think Susan is old enough to be on birth control? She's only fourteen for Christ's sake."

"You're acting like she's on birth control so she can go around having sex with everyone."

Thoroughly confused, Vincent walked to the kitchen table and sat down. "I don't understand," he said. "Why else would she go on birth control?"

"It helps her with her period, something she's not exactly comfortable talking to you about. Pills help with cramps and stuff. You'd think as someone who does as much research and writing as you would know about that."

"I write crime novels, Lillian, not chick lit."

Lillian rolled her eyes and turned her back to him. Agreeing that their dialogue was over, Vincent got up from the table and stalked out of the kitchen. There was no part of the conversation that did not disturb him. He was ashamed that his own wife kept such a secret from him. She didn't think he cared about Susan or Neil. This was an accusation that had been thrown at him numerous times over the past few days, and Vincent began to wonder if there was any validity behind the statement.

He quickly dismissed the idea when he thought about how bothered he got when reading about Susan. Only a caring father would react similarly to something so offensive toward his child.

Still, now that he knew the part about Susan being on birth control turned out to be true, Vincent grew even more worried about the rest of the manuscript. He was hoping Lillian would tell him there was no way Susan could be on the pill. Unfortunately, he found himself getting more and more surprised by the people he thought he knew.

Vincent began to slowly make his way up the stairs. He knew there was one more thing to do to confirm the truth of Kevin Larre's writing. And, it was something he'd been dreading all morning. His conversation with Lillian did nothing to ease his suspicions of Susan, and he needed to find out about his daughter, no matter how much it might hurt.

Vincent walked through the hallway lined with family photos. Each picture showed smiling faces, smiles that were as false as his mother's dreams of success.

Vincent pushed open the door to his daughter's room. Looking around, he took in the sights of a seemingly normal bedroom of a fourteen-year-old girl. Posters of actors and singers he couldn't identify, a laptop with a photo slideshow screensaver, a closet whose doors couldn't close all the way because of the overabundance of clothes and shoes. One glance at the room produced no troubling notions of the girl who lived in it.

Inching closer to the bed, Vincent tried to prepare himself for what he was sure he would find underneath it. After a few seconds of meditating on the edge of Susan's pink bedspread, he leaned over and reached underneath. He came back up holding a black and purple shoebox. He felt dizzy holding it in his lap. He felt like he was holding Pandora's Box, and he was about to unleash a whole slew of demons.

Without any other choice, Vincent lifted the lid and peeked inside.

It was past eight o'clock when Susan walked into the house. She went to the kitchen to grab a bottle of coke from the fridge before heading up to her room. When she entered her bedroom, she didn't expect to see her father pacing and her mother sitting on the bed crying.

"What's going on?" she asked.

"Susan! How could you?" Lillian exclaimed.

"What are you talking about?"

"Sit down," Vincent said sternly.

Susan looked terrified when she went to her desk chair to sit down. She couldn't imagine what she'd done or what her parents could possibly be so upset about.

That is until Vincent walked over and threw photos down on the desk in front of her. Her eyes widened when she saw what they were photos of. Her with Sean. Her with James. With Andrew. With Steve. With John. With Phil. With Craig.

Susan burst into tears. "I'm sorry! I'm so sorry!"

"How long has this been going on?" Lillian demanded.

"I never meant for you to find out," Susan said. "How did you find out?"

Vincent looked at her disgustedly. "It doesn't make a difference how we found out."

"I know you're shocked," Susan replied. "But it's not like I wasn't safe. I'm on the pill."

"And it never occurred to you that what you were doing was illegal?"

Susan looked at her mother questioningly. "What do you mean? What's illegal about what I did?"

"It's one thing to sleep around at your age," answered Lillian, "but to sell yourself? To *prostitute* yourself?"

The word prostitute shocked Susan to her very core. "Prostitute? What are you talking about?"

Vincent walked up to her again and this time threw down letters and a large pile of money. "We mean, my dear, the fact that along with the photos, there was also seven hundred dollars and plenty of letters thanking you for your services."

Susan stared down at the letters and cash, completely flabbergasted. There was no way for her to contain her shock.

"I swear," she stuttered, "I have *never* seen these letters before. And, I certainly never got any cash."

"Are we supposed to believe you?" said Vincent.

"Dad, I'm not lying."

"I find that hard to believe."

"It's true."

"Then where did the money come from?" Lillian chimed in.

"I don't know!" Susan cried.

"After all that we've given you," Vincent yelled, "you go and whore yourself out!"

Susan once again burst into tears. Lillian immediately followed suit. Not able to take anymore of this, Vincent stormed out of the room in utter disgust. He headed down the stairs and out the front door. A drive seemed like the only escape for him at the moment.

The envelope lying next to the front tire of his car, however, did nothing to temper his anger.

SIXTEEN

Marital Status

Long, curly black hair with streaks of amber blew out the open window of the red Corvette as it sped around the corner. Lillian did not like being late to anything, especially outings with friends. Her purse, which occupied the passenger seat, flew forward as she slammed on the brakes to avoid rear-ending the Highlander in front of her.

Glancing at the clock on the dashboard, Lillian let out a high pitched squeal: 12:37. She was already seven minutes late, and she knew it would take her at least another twenty minutes to get to the tennis club. She was anxious to finally get there and relieve some of the stress from her hectic daily life. Between her husband and her restaurant, there was hardly any time left for her to enjoy time to herself and with her friends.

God, sometimes Vincent made her so angry. He actually complained about his milk this morning. She wasn't his slave. She didn't marry him so she could run errands for him all the time. Why did she marry him? She was pretty sure it was for love. Why else would she have married him twenty-three years ago?

When she met him at Club Mayhem all those years ago, she immediately saw his potential to become a great writer, and he had seen her potential to become a great chef. She thought it would be so romantic to be married to a writer. And, it was at first. By the time Neil was born, however, she was beginning to feel more like a necessity in his life rather than someone he wanted. She felt he loved the idea of her more than he really loved her, leaving her depressed and angry.

She desperately needed this friendly excursion after that morning's uncomfortable breakfast encounter with Vincent. She found herself getting less and less capable of dealing with his self-obsessed attitude.

She reached over to pick up her purse as her wallet, lipstick, compact, and several tampons spilled onto the floor mat. Taking advantage of the red light, Lillian leaned over and scooped up the clutter. By the time she had everything back in order, the light had turned green. She leaned on her horn to wake up the driver of the Highlander who didn't seem to notice the light switch.

Lillian sped past the slow traffic when the single lane road split into two lanes. She reached over to her cell phone which she kept in the cup holder. Without taking her eyes off the road, she flipped it open and held down the number "3" until the phone indicated it was calling Franci.

"Come on, Franci. Answer your phone," Lillian grumbled. The dash clock now read 12:42. Lillian turned down the volume of her radio in order to better hear her friend when she finally answered the phone.

"You're already twelve minutes late. I'm in shock."

Lillian smiled, unable to be in any kind of bad mood when talking to Franci. Francis Tuppletin had been Lillian's best friend ever since Francis had stormed into the kitchen of La Lemoné and complained that her 32-ounce t-bone wasn't rare enough. Lillian had been head chef at La Lemoné for nearly two years at that time, and never had a customer complaint been so amusing to her. Just the fact that a four-foot-eleven-inch woman without an ounce of fat on her had the audacity to order a 32-ounce piece of meat was enough to send chuckles through Lillian's equally thin frame.

"Yeah, well, I had an emergency errand to run," said Lillian, glad her friend wasn't mad at her tardiness.

"An emergency? I hope it wasn't serious."

"No, no. Perhaps emergency is too strong a word. It was stupid really. I'll explain when I get there. I'll probably be another ten minutes."

"Alright, no problem. I'll just sit here and admire the cute guy behind the counter in the café."

Lillian hung up and gripped the wheel in frustration. She hated being late. Punctuality was always high on her list. She would have to buy Franci a nice lunch to make it up to her.

Lillian turned to look in the back seat. She wanted to make sure that her gym bag and tennis racket were with her. She would hate to finally get to the club only to realize she didn't have her clothes and racket.

By the time she arrived at Rockaway Tennis Club, it was 1:02. Lillian reached into the backseat and grabbed her things, not bothering to get out and actually open the back door. With purse and gym bag slung over her shoulder, she raced to the entrance of the club. She found Franci sitting on a stool pretending to read a newspaper while subtly catching glimpses of Andre, the twenty-four year old waiter who served the best crullers in Rockaway.

Lillian snuck up behind her friend and leaned toward her ear. "You do know you're over twice his age, right?"

Franci chuckled as she spun around in her seat to face Lillian. "Yeah, well, I don't think I look that old."

"That's true," replied Lillian. And, it was true. Franci still looked like she could be in her mid-thirties, a great compliment for someone who just celebrated the big five-oh. Her blonde hair was cut short so it perfectly framed her petite face. "Maybe, you should remember your husband."

"Always killing my fun, aren't you?" Franci smiled and jumped off the stool before giving Lillian a hug and peck on each cheek. "Shall we play?"

"By all means." The two women waltzed to the women's locker room to change before their weekly ritual of lobbing balls haphazardly on the indoor tennis courts of the club. Lillian and Franci both knew they lacked any kind of talent when it came to tennis, but they enjoyed the activity, nonetheless.

When they found their usual lockers, they set their belongings down on the bench. Lillian proceeded to unzip her bag, but Franci just stood there, smiling a big cheesy smile.

"What?" asked Lillian, cocking her left eyebrow inquisitively.

Franci waved her newspaper in Lillian's face. "I thought you'd be interested in what I was reading."

"Really? Something exciting?"

"I'd say so." Franci sat down on the bench and motioned for Lillian to follow suit. Lillian obeyed as Franci flipped through the newspaper until she found the proper page. Lillian looked down and scrunched her face.

"Oh yeah," she said. "I guess I forgot to tell you."

"You're always supposed to let me know when you're getting reviewed. That way I can show up, get a table near the critic, and make yummy noises." Franci gave Lillian a look of fake disappointment before returning her gaze to the review. "Of course it looks like you didn't need me there this time."

Lillian took the paper from Franci and skimmed the article. Words and phrases like "brilliant combination" and "heavenly" jumped out at her, making her smile. "Oh shoot. I only got three and a half stars. Must be the busboy's fault," said Lillian with a slight giggle.

"Well, if you want the other half of that star, don't forget to call me next time." Franci raised her eyebrows and observed her well-manicured fingernails in an attempt to look snooty. She couldn't quite pull it off.

"I'll remember that," said Lillian as she flipped to the next page. She found herself staring at more reviews of theater and books. As her eyes moved down the page, they eventually settled on an outstanding book review.

Vincent Kraver delivers another page turner with his novel* Quiet Thunder. *Its intricate combination of deceit, warfare, and espionage make his latest thriller number one in readers' opinions. When foreign diplomat Owen MacAlister receives a ransom note demanding the United States' plans for an underwater industrial habitat in exchange for his fourteen-year-old niece, he must become a spy for both America and its

secret enemy, Scandinavia. It isn't until a startling discovery of the young girl's genius leaks out that Owen must determine who the real enemy is, and who is truly demanding the ransom. **Quiet Thunder** *will keep your mind engaged in political and scientific puzzles from cover to cover.*

Lillian put the paper down and stared up at Franci. "Well, it sounds like my husband wrote another masterpiece. Maybe, I should find time to read it."

Franci picked up on the sarcasm in her friend's voice and took a seat next to Lillian on the bench. "Are things not getting any better?"

Lillian shook her head. "I thought they would since he finished the book. You know how he gets when he's deep in writing mode."

"Sure," replied Franci, waiting for Lillian to continue.

"I thought maybe he'd open up to me and the kids more, but he seems just as self-absorbed at before."

"But, I thought you said he's been like this since you met him."

"He has, but I guess when I first met him, he seemed more mysterious and interesting than just self-absorbed."

"If you're this unhappy why don't you talk to him about it?"

"I try, but our arguments always end with me or him storming out. Like this morning, he complained about not having any more of his milk left. I had to run to the store and pick some up before I came here."

"Wait," interrupted Franci. "Was that the emergency errand you had to run?" Lillian answered with a tiny nod. "Wow."

"Yeah. He's a brilliant man, but he can be such a baby."

"Are you only putting up with him because you think he's brilliant?"

"Well, he has some good moments. And, there are the children to think about."

Franci paused for a few seconds, carefully considering how to word her next sentence. "Lillian, honey, I know how much you hate the 'D' word, but..."

"No," Lillian interrupted. "Divorce is not an option."

"You can't stay together just for the kids."

"Yes we can. Besides, Susan just started high school. I wouldn't even consider separating until both Neil and Susan have left for college."

"But, that's another four years."

"Four years isn't that long."

Franci looked at Lillian, not bothering to hide the pity in her eyes.

"Okay," said Lillian. "This conversation got kind of depressing. Let's go knock a few balls around."

The women proceeded to change into their tennis clothes with the unease of their conversation still lingering in the stagnant air of the locker room. Lillian's thoughts continued, however, as she tried to think of a solution to ease the next four years of her life.

SEVENTEEN

Vincent woke up early the next morning with a sore back and a headache that would disable even the strongest of men. He'd spent the night tossing and turning, not able to get the disgusting images of his daughter with all those boys out of his head. Never in a million years would he have suspected Susan of doing something so low and degrading.

And, what about what he'd read about Lillian? Was she really that unhappy? She certainly had some nerve complaining to Franci rather than talking to him directly. He deserved more respect than that. Even if Lillian was upset, there was nothing that could be worse than what they had learned about his devious daughter.

Sitting up slowly, Vincent felt even more miserable. It seemed like his back and his head were competing to see who could cause him the most pain. It was a pointless competition, however, since nothing could beat the pain he felt from Susan's actions.

Vincent wanted more than anything for the information to be false. All the evidence made the truth undeniable. If it weren't for the letters and the cash, Vincent would have certainly believed his daughter. Unfortunately, there was no point in trying to believe anything she said.

Vincent forced himself out of bed, knowing that wallowing in his grief would be a waste of time. Lillian's side of the bed was vacant. She must have had trouble sleeping just like him. Most likely she was down in the kitchen cooking up a storm. That was her usual way of dealing with stress and anxiety.

The bathroom was cold and uninviting. That seemed to be the personality of everything in Vincent's life lately. He opened the window curtain and peered outside. The backyard usually provided a pretty picture, but dark clouds and howling winds marred the beautiful landscape. A slight drizzle began to fall. Vincent thought it was weird how often the weather mirrored the atmosphere in his home.

The hot shower did nothing to dull the pain in Vincent's muscles. He stepped out of the shower feeling no better than when he got in. No matter what he did, he could not get the situation with Susan out of his head.

Vincent got dressed and headed downstairs hoping to talk with Lillian. Things had clearly been strenuous between them lately. The latest manuscript chapter proved that. But, Vincent hoped the incident from last night would allow them to talk calmly with each other and work as a team. It was unfortunate that it took the discovery of such a horrible secret to get a husband and wife to talk to each other.

It seemed a talk with Lillian was not going to happen that morning, however. Vincent walked into a dark and empty kitchen. There was a note taped to the fridge:

Vincent, couldn't get my mind off of things. Went to run some errands before work. Be back late. Lillian

"Well, that makes two of us," he said as he crumpled the note and threw it in the trash under the sink. Vincent thought about making himself breakfast but found he didn't have much of an appetite.

He headed back upstairs to tape a note and some money to Neil's door. The note said he needed to borrow his car again, and the money was for a cab to and from school.

After finding the keys to his son's car, Vincent proceeded out the door. He started driving without any destination in mind. It was nearly December, and Vincent gladly welcomed the cold weather. He lowered the windows to create a breeze. The cool air helped rid him of his headache and partially clear his boggled mind.

He stopped at a red light and thought about the direction he wanted to go. He sat for several minutes, letting the light change from red to green to yellow and back to red. At 5:27 in the morning, there was no one else on the road for him to bother.

The light once again turned green, and Vincent turned left, finally knowing where he wanted to go. The issue with Susan would not stop nagging at him until he talked it through with someone. He had hoped to talk to Lillian, but as usual, she made herself unavailable to him. As his life seemed to be getting more and more hectic, Vincent found himself with fewer people to turn to for help.

Of course, before this week, Vincent had rarely needed help. He was always self-sufficient and relied on himself to solve his own problems. Growing up with Janet Kraver had taught him this was the only way to survive in the world. He could certainly never rely on his mother to help him with anything, let alone give him useful advice on any topic.

After a few minutes of driving down barren streets, Vincent pulled into the driveway of a large house. It wasn't as big as his, but it was still rather sizeable compared to the rest of the houses in the neighborhood. He looked to a window on the top floor and was happy to see a light was on.

Vincent walked up to the front door and rang the bell. He could hear the melodic chime echo throughout the large house. The outside was completely silent with the exception of leaves rustling with the movement of birds who opted out of migrating this year.

After a few minutes, Vincent saw the light come on in the foyer. Patrick answered the door in his bathrobe.

"Vincent!" he exclaimed, very surprised to see his old friend. The volume of Patrick's voice startled Vincent who had gotten used to the quiet of the morning.

"Hi, Pat. Sorry to drop by so early. Can I come in?"

"Y-yeah, sure. C-c-come in." Patrick never stuttered, and Vincent wondered why he was acting so nervous. Maybe, he was confusing nervousness with bewilderment. After all, it wasn't often that Vincent visited Patrick at his home. He certainly never came by at such an early hour, and never unannounced.

Now that he thought about it, Patrick was probably worried that something was terribly wrong. *Isn't there?* Vincent thought, the issue with Susan once more popping into his head.

Patrick led Vincent into his living room. "I'll be right back," he said as he rushed up the stairs. Vincent looked around the room and noticed there were no photos anywhere. He wondered why Patrick had never found a woman and settled down. Of the two of them, Vincent would have chosen Pat as the more likely one to get married and start a family.

Instead, Vincent was the lucky one to end up with a wife and kids. Well, maybe lucky wasn't the right word for what he ended up with, at least not lately.

Patrick came back down the stairs a little more relaxed. He still seemed a bit on edge, however. He sat down for two seconds before popping back up.

“Would you like some coffee? I’ll make some coffee.”

Before Vincent could answer, Patrick was already out of the living room and in the kitchen. After a few minutes, he returned from the kitchen and sat down.

“Are you okay?” Vincent asked.

“Yeah, I’m fine,” Patrick replied. “I’m usually like this in the morning.”

“Maybe, you should see a psychologist about that.” Vincent smiled at his weak attempt at a joke. Patrick didn’t seem to pick up on it.

“So, what are you doing here? It’s not even six yet. Is everything okay?”

“Well, I know you don’t have your first patient until eight o’clock, and I was wondering if you could fit me in before that.”

“Sure,” Patrick answered. “What’s the problem?”

Vincent wasn’t sure of the proper way to bring it up, so he chose the most straightforward approach.

“Susan is sleeping with boys at her school…for money.”

Patrick’s eyes nearly bulged from their sockets. “Excuse me?”

“I found erotic pictures of Susan with many different boys from her school. Hundreds of them.”

“How does that mean prostitution?”

"There were also letters thanking her for her services."

"That still doesn't mean…"

"And, seven hundred dollars."

"Oh." After taking a few minutes to let the information sink in, Patrick continued. "Are you going to confront her?"

"We already did."

"We?"

"Me and Lillian."

"How did Lillian react?"

Vincent sat back against the soft cushion of the couch. "She's devastated, of course. She barely even looked at Susan when we talked to her. I wanted to talk to Lillian about it this morning, but she was gone before I even woke up. She left a note saying she was running errands, though I can't imagine where she'd go. I mean, what's open this early in the morning?"

"Right," Patrick replied, shifting uncomfortably in his spot on the couch.

"Are you sure you're okay?" Vincent asked.

"Yeah. So, what did Susan say?"

Vincent decided to ignore Patrick's erratic behavior. "She's denying the whole thing. Says she never sold her body to anyone. She has no idea where the cash or letters came from. She's never seen them before in her life."

"Could she be telling the truth?"

"Where else could the money have come from?"

Patrick rubbed his eyes like he was still waking up. "Oh! The coffee!" he shouted, once again startling Vincent. Patrick jumped up and made his way back to the kitchen. He returned with two steaming cups of coffee.

Vincent was about to take a sip when Patrick asked a rather idiotic question. "How do you feel about all this?"

"Oh, I'm overjoyed. Couldn't be more thrilled."

Now Patrick looked annoyed. "It's barely after six in the morning. You woke me up to talk and you're being sarcastic?"

You weren't asleep. Your bedroom light was on when I drove up. Vincent kept his thought to himself. "Sorry."

An awkward silence passed while they each took long sips from their mugs.

"I just don't understand it," Vincent continued. "She's only fourteen years old."

"Believe me, that has nothing to do with anything," Patrick replied.

"What do you mean?"

"I have a lot of teenage patients, and the majority of their problems are sexual in nature."

"Why?"

"Those are the years when hormones wake up and start going crazy. It's completely natural for sexual appetites to increase dramatically in middle school, and especially in high school."

"Yeah," said Vincent, "but there were more than a few boys. This isn't sexual exploration. It's more like sexual obsession. There must have been at least a hundred guys."

"Maybe, she's filling a vacant spot in her life."

Vincent looked at Patrick waiting for him to carry on. "What do you mean?" he asked when Pat took too long to continue.

"Think about it, Vincent. What is the one thing Susan lacks in her life?"

Vincent thought about what Susan could possibly be missing from her life. He gave her everything a teenage girl required to survive in today's world. Every luxury that daughters beg their fathers for--a cell phone, a television, clothes, shoes, food, and a house to die for. "I don't know," Vincent finally answered.

"She doesn't have many, if any, male figures in her life."

"That's ridiculous. She lives with me, and Neil's bedroom is right next to hers."

"Yes, but you still don't offer much of a presence. You're never there. So, she may be seeking male approval because she doesn't get it at home."

Something was triggered in Vincent's memory, but he didn't want to let Patrick know what he was thinking. He turned to look out the window and hide his expression from his friend. "What do you mean?" He hoped that the anxiety couldn't be heard in his voice.

"The truth is you work a lot. You don't spend much quality time with Susan. It's important for a girl to have a strong relationship with her father to feel complete, and you don't have much free time. And, Neil doesn't pay much attention to her either, except to drive her to school every day.

"With you and Neil constantly out of the picture, it's very possible that she turns to other boys for male approval. And, unfortunately, the most certifiable way to gain male approval from boys her age is to give herself to them sexually."

Vincent took a moment to absorb Patrick's words. Basically, Patrick was telling him that it was mostly his fault, and partly Neil's, that Susan turned into a fourteen-year-old prostitute. He came here expecting to gain a little comfort from his old friend, but instead he felt insulted and even more apprehensive than before.

"So, what do you suggest I do?" he asked.

"The best, and probably only solution, is family therapy. You should do your best to keep your family together during this crisis."

"Yeah, that's why I came to you. I don't want my family to fall apart. And, when I woke up and found Lillian gone, I had no one else to turn to."

"Well, you're always welcome to stop by," said Patrick rising from the couch. "Unfortunately, though, I *do* need to prepare for my sessions and make a few calls."

"Okay, I'll leave. Thanks for the advice."

"Anytime."

Vincent stood up and offered his hand for a handshake. Pat shook it, still looking on edge. "Do you mind if I use your bathroom before I leave?"

"Uh, yeah. No problem. Sorry, but I really need to head upstairs."

"Okay. I'll let myself out."

"Okay. See you later, Vince."

"Bye." Patrick charged up the stairs as if he had a bomb to dismantle. He never saw his friend move to get away from him so quickly.

Vincent made his way to the bathroom located near the front door. After closing the door, he lowered the lid of the toilet and sat down. He rested his head between his knees and took a few deep breaths. He couldn't believe what he just heard Patrick say. Could he have heard him wrong? Could he be looking too much into it?

It wasn't what he said about Susan needing therapy that upset him. Vincent already knew it was probably the only solution to the problem.

No, it was when Patrick mentioned Susan's search for male approval that prompted a memory that put Vincent on edge. Vincent remembered reading that same reason for Susan's behavior in the pages sent to him by Kevin Larre. What were the chances that Patrick would come up with the same exact motivation for Susan's promiscuity as Kevin Larre did in the manuscript? Vincent had never told Patrick about the documents he had been receiving, yet he managed to repeat to Vincent what he had read last night.

Patrick was certainly acting very strange this morning. Vincent had never seen him behave so agitated. Why was he so jumpy? Why did he seem so eager to get Vincent out of his house? Was Patrick the author of the manuscripts? Was Patrick Donway the true identity of Kevin Larre? Vincent came here for answers, and instead, he found himself leaving with even more questions.

Vincent flushed the toilet and splashed water on his face. He walked out of the bathroom and heard movement upstairs. Figuring Patrick was busy getting ready for work, Vincent didn't bother calling out to say goodbye.

He opened the front door and headed down the steps. The large yellow envelope stood out like an eyesore on the stone walkway. Assuming it was for him, Vincent bent over to pick up the delivery. His assumption was confirmed when he saw his name on the envelope and a photograph glued to the corner.

There was something even more alarming about this delivery than all the previous ones. The picture in the corner was taken with a Polaroid camera. It was of Patrick's house with Neil's car parked in the driveway. The back of Vincent's head could be seen through the large window separating Patrick's living room from the cold outside. Whoever made the delivery managed to snap a quick shot of Patrick's house, probably no more than five minutes ago, and drop off the envelope without being seen.

Vincent looked up and down the street but saw no other cars. Making a quick decision, Vincent ran to the car and sped out of the driveway. If the manuscript was delivered only minutes ago, there was a chance he could catch up with whomever dropped it off. Vincent ignored the stop sign at the corner of the street to chase…someone. Exactly who he was chasing, he had no idea.

Patrick peered through his bedroom curtains. Relief didn't come until he saw Vincent speed out of his driveway and disappear around the corner. For once, he was thankful his guest parked in the garage. He didn't know what he would have done if Vincent found out they were not the only two in his house during this unexpected visit.

EIGHTEEN

It was six-thirty in the morning and Vincent never felt more awake or alert. The roads were more populated than when he drove to Patrick's house just an hour earlier. It looked like his hunt for whomever left the envelope on Pat's front walkway would be unsuccessful.

On his way home, Vincent passed the crowded parking lot of a diner. He never would have thought a diner would be so popular at such an early hour during the week. After driving half a block, Vincent decided to turn around and get a meal at the diner. He had no plans for the day, and he felt too anxious to go home. Neil was probably still upset, and Vincent was not ready to face Susan. He wondered if he'd ever be ready.

Vincent pulled into the diner parking lot. There were already people leaving the restaurant after early breakfasts. A blinking sign over the entrance indicated the diner was open 24 hours.

The host led Vincent to a small table by a window. Vincent ordered a coffee when his waitress walked over. A small hum of conversations could be heard throughout the restaurant.

Vincent looked at the envelope he brought in with him. The temptation to open it and read its contents was almost overwhelming. But, the fear was even stronger than the curiosity.

The last time he opened an envelope, he learned his daughter was whoring herself out to her classmates. Actually, the manuscript never indicated Susan received money, but the cash under her bed along with the letters was clear. Maybe, Kevin Larre wasn't aware of everything, but his manuscript led Vincent to discover his daughter's dirty and illegal secret.

The thought of Susan selling her body to hundreds of boys made Vincent's stomach churn. He thumbed the corner of the envelope debating whether or not to open it. The waitress ended his silent deliberation when she came over to take his order. Vincent didn't have the stomach to learn anything new about his family. He put the envelope aside and ordered toast. Nothing else seemed especially appetizing to him at the moment.

Vincent watched his waitress walk away and let his gaze travel around the rest of the diner to observe the other patrons. That's when an unnerving thought suddenly occurred to him. What if Kevin Larre was in the diner with him? Up until now, the mysterious author had been able to reveal things to Vincent that could only be detected with extreme surveillance.

And, Kevin Larre also knew he was at Patrick's house that morning, and his mother's assisted-living facility two nights before. He knew when he'd be at his book signings as well. Kevin Larre was clearly keeping a close eye on Vincent. Was it possible he was here now, grabbing an early breakfast along with all the others in the diner this morning?

"Would you like anything else?"

Vincent was lost in thought and didn't notice his waitress put his order down in front of him.

"No, thank you," he responded. Vincent realized he was being paranoid. Kevin Larre couldn't have known he would stop at the diner on his way home. Vincent didn't even know he'd be here. The manuscripts were starting to bring out a side of Vincent's personality that he didn't know existed. If he wasn't careful, they would eventually turn him into someone who constantly looked over his shoulder and was suspicious of everyone. The only way to make sure that didn't happen was to stop reading the manuscripts. However, Vincent knew more than anyone that his curiosity would never let that happen.

Vincent slowly buttered his toast, suddenly feeling very tired. He no longer had any idea how to go about discovering the identity of Kevin Larre. Of course, he didn't really have any ideas before this either. Why was this man able to evade Vincent so easily? If nothing else, Vincent always believed himself to be an extremely sharp-eyed person, keenly aware of his surroundings. Nothing ever happened around Vincent Kraver without him being fully conscious of it. It's what made him able to write such successful novels. Vincent knew people and situations because he walked through the world with his eyes wide open. Nothing escaped him. *Ever*.

As if trying to prove this to himself, Vincent looked around the diner to scrutinize everything and everyone around him. A few tables away from his, the host was seating a family of four. A mother led a young girl by the hand while the son and father followed. The father was dressed for work in a navy suit and light-blue tie with snowflakes peppered on it. It looked like the kind of tie given to him by his children for Father's Day or Christmas.

The mother removed her daughter's puffy pink coat before removing her own jacket and taking a seat in the booth. Both children appeared sleepy and were still in their pajama bottoms. The host set children's menus and crayons in front of the youngsters before walking away.

While the grownups perused their menus, the brother and sister set to coloring on their placemats and solving the easy word searches and connect-the-dots. They didn't look up when the waitress came over to ask what they wanted to drink. Their mother ordered apple juice for both of them, a cup of coffee for herself, and the father requested a coffee and a small cranberry juice.

The waitress returned a few minutes later with their drinks and took out her pad to write down their food orders. The father ordered pancakes for his children who were still engrossed in their coloring. He then asked for omelets for him and his wife and a side of bacon for them to share. The waitress gave them a friendly smile before returning to the kitchen.

The family passed the time waiting for their breakfasts by playing tic-tac-toe. The mother and daughter teamed up against the father and son. It was really more of a battle between the brother and sister while the parents offered encouragement and smiled at each other over the heads of their two children.

By the time the sixth game had ended, the boy had won four while the girl only won two. In truth, the boy let his younger sister win both times. He didn't want her to feel bad.

The food was delivered in the midst of their seventh game. The mother and father cut up their children's pancakes to give them time to finish playing. While they ate, the children asked their father about his upcoming business trip. He was going to California for a week to attend some important meetings. The daughter made him promise to call her every night before she went to bed and then proceeded to eat her breakfast in silence.

The family looked sad while they ate. Vincent believed that the father tried hard to stay home as much as possible, but some business trips were impossible to get out of. He missed his family dearly when he was away, and they missed him just as much.

When everyone finished eating, the foursome rose from their table to leave. The brother held his sister's hand while they walked to the front of the diner. Their parents followed close behind them with their arms wrapped tightly around each other.

After paying the bill, the father walked his wife and kids to a silver minivan. He picked up each child individually and gave them giant hugs along with multiple kisses. He whispered something to each of them before putting them down and letting them crawl into the van. After the vehicle's doors were shut with the children securely inside, the husband and wife embraced for a full minute, each not wanting to be the first to let go. They kissed and said goodbye after promises to call each other every day. The woman then got in the driver's seat of the van while the man walked over to another car. When they drove out of the parking lot, the vehicles went in separate directions, leaving a family that would not feel complete again until the following week.

Vincent watched this family while thinking of his own. Rarely did his line of work take him out of town, except for a book signing every few years. As a writer, he spent most of his time working at home. Yet he felt a constant detachment from his wife and kids. He thought about the upcoming weeks when he'd be across the country and wondered if his family would miss him. Whenever he went on a trip, he was never embraced like the man he'd just seen in the diner. Vincent had strong doubts that his family ever missed him when he was gone.

There was certainly never any closeness between Neil and Susan like Vincent saw between the two children. They never played tic-tac-toe together. They definitely never held hands.

The family Vincent saw in the diner that morning was one he never knew existed in real life. He had written about some like that in his novels, but only as ways to reveal the harsher realities his main characters lived in. This was the first time Vincent realized this type of family truly did exist. A family where they loved each other and missed each other when they weren't together.

Was Vincent's family anything like that? Vincent couldn't remember the last time he ate with his family and a fight didn't erupt. He couldn't remember the last time he and his family decided to go out for a nice dinner together. The saddest thing, however, was that Vincent couldn't remember the last time he and Lillian smiled at each other from across the table.

"Sir, can I get you something else?"

Vincent looked up at the waitress and shook his head. "Just the check." He didn't realize how long he'd been sitting there. The waitress looked slightly confused from having served a man only coffee and toast, yet he stayed for forty-five minutes. Vincent felt like he was confusing everyone he came in contact with lately.

After leaving a generous tip, Vincent walked to the front to pay. Under his arm, he carried the envelope still sealed. He was relieved that there was nothing new waiting for him when he got in the car.

Vincent threw the envelope in the front seat and prepared to drive home. Instead of turning left out of the parking lot, however, he turned right, away from his mansion. All he wanted to do today was drive and clear his head. So, that's what he did. Without any destination in mind, Vincent drove.

NINETEEN

It wasn't until after dark that Vincent finally got home. He was exhausted from driving for hours with no direction. What was supposed to clear his head only left him feeling tired and even more lost.

He still hadn't read the manuscript. He was sure whatever Kevin Larre had to say would only add to his already depressed mood.

Vincent reached his office door and was about to unlock it when Lillian came rushing down the hall.

"Where the hell have you been? I've tried calling you all day."

"Really?" Vincent responded as he took his cell phone out of his pocket. "I didn't hear my phone ring." Vincent flipped open his phone and realized it had been turned off all day.

Lillian started talking again before he could explain. "Where were you? I called Patrick and he said you were at his house early this morning. He said you were talking about Susan."

"Yeah, I wanted to talk things over with you this morning, but you were gone when I woke up. By the way, where do you go for errands at five-thirty in the morning?"

“What did Patrick say about Susan?” Lillian asked, completely ignoring his question. Vincent was too tired to wheedle an answer out of her as to her location.

“He said family therapy is the only solution. I don’t see anything else that we can do.” Lillian remained silent. “He also thinks she could be telling the truth about not getting money from boys.”

“Oh, please!” she exclaimed. “How else can she explain the cash we found? It’s not like we can talk to her anymore about it. She never came home after school.”

“Where is she?”

“Neil said she went to Lauren’s house. She can stay there for the rest of her life for all I care.” Vincent winced at his wife’s harsh words. Lillian was usually the first one in line to defend Susan. Now, she wasn’t even giving her daughter a chance. “Are you going to tell me where you were today?” The tone of Lillian’s question sounded very accusatory.

“I didn’t go anywhere,” Vincent replied. “I just drove around all day.” Lillian clearly didn’t believe him, but Vincent knew it was the truth.

“Fine,” she said tersely. “I’m going to bed.” Lillian turned and headed toward the stairs without saying goodnight. When Vincent thought about it, he realized his wife hadn’t said goodnight to him in a long time.

Vincent unlocked his office and went in. He made sure to lock it before going to his desk. He didn't want any more intrusions that night.

He sat in his chair at the big mahogany desk. He laid the envelope in front of him, and its yellow color stood out against the rich color of the wood. He still hadn't looked in the envelope. Now he had two options: open it now or lay awake in bed all night wondering what's inside.

Making up his mind, Vincent grabbed a letter opener from his top drawer and opened the package. To his surprise, the chapter he was looking at now was much shorter than the others he'd been receiving. Vincent silently wished this meant there was less chance of it revealing another horrible secret. Unfortunately, there was only one way to find out.

Adjusting his glasses on the bridge of his nose, Vincent lifted the manuscript and began to read.

Growing Suspicions

Vincent was utterly at a loss about what he should do about his family. He knew he had to find Kevin Larre and discover how and where he was getting the information for his manuscripts.

But accomplishing that difficult task would not solve the problems that Vincent had recently discovered about his

family. Whether Kevin Larre was the one to tell him, or if it was someone else entirely, his family would still have the same problems.

The morning after confronting Susan about her illegal sexual activities, Vincent had hoped to talk to Lillian and try to come up with a solution for their daughter. His wife's absence, however, made that rather difficult. Vincent was left by himself, something he was actually growing quite used to.

Without anyone else to turn to, Vincent went to his friend Patrick's house for an unexpected visit. He thought if anyone could provide any wisdom regarding his family crisis, it would be his psychologist friend. The visit, however, turned out to be considerably confusing and uncomfortable for the old friends. Nothing seemed to be making any sense lately, and the oddity of Patrick's behavior only added to the growing pot of questions Vincent had about his life and everyone in it.

Vincent paused for a few seconds and thought about what he was reading. This chapter must have been written before he went to Patrick's house in order for it to have been delivered during his visit. But, how did Kevin Larre know he would visit his friend that day? How did he know Lillian wouldn't be there for him to talk to that morning?

The person who was Kevin Larre obviously knew Vincent very well. He knew he'd turn to Patrick for advice when Lillian wasn't around. And, somehow, he knew Lillian would not be around that morning, leaving Vincent no other choice but to drive to Patrick's house.

Still unsure, Vincent continued reading.

Vincent walked out of Patrick's house with more questions than when he'd arrived. How was it possible that nothing in Vincent's life was making any sense? Vincent considered himself intelligent and alert. Nothing got by him easily.

Just as he was thinking this, Vincent saw another envelope lying on the ground outside Patrick's house. He knew it was for him before he even picked it up because of the picture glued to the corner. A picture of Patrick's house with a view of Vincent through the window sitting on the couch in the living room.

Vincent looked around hoping to catch a glimpse of whoever dropped off the envelope. Unfortunately, he (or she) was already gone. This didn't stop him from running to his car in hopes of catching up to his stalker, if that was even the proper label for Kevin Larre. His pursuit, however, yielded no

rewards or answers for Vincent. He continued driving for hours, chasing no one and finding out absolutely nothing.

At least he didn't know I'd go to the diner, Vincent thought. Still, Kevin Larre knew Vincent well. Too well. He knew Vincent wouldn't go directly home after visiting Patrick. Anyone who could predict his moves that accurately would have to have been watching Vincent very closely for a long time now.

The thought of someone watching him and learning his habits sent a chill up Vincent's spine. He finally decided that he had to call the police. He felt threatened, both physically and psychologically.

Vincent got up from his desk, still holding on to the manuscript, and walked over to the phone. He skimmed the rest of the chapter while he walked. As he was about to dial the police, though, he read a paragraph that made him pause.

Lillian approached Vincent when he finally arrived home late that night. She questioned him anxiously about where he'd been all day. Her apprehension seemed more like suspicion of his whereabouts rather than concern.

Vincent was never one to stay out all day, so it was no wonder that his wife questioned where he'd gone and who he'd been with. He reassured her that he spent all day driving

around, not going anywhere. Lillian's unease about Vincent's actions that day was not lessened by his answer. Deciding not to take the issue any further, Lillian headed off to bed, leaving Vincent standing alone outside his office.

Vincent entered his office thinking about finally reading the manuscript he'd been carrying around with him like a heavy weight all day. What he should have been thinking about, however, was that while Lillian was acting suspicious of his actions all day, maybe Vincent should be even more suspicious of *her* actions.

Was that it? Vincent flipped the page over, but there was no more written. He went to check the envelope, which he threw on his desk. There were no more pages to this chapter.

What was being hidden from Vincent Kraver? Why did Kevin Larre suggest he be suspicious of Lillian but not explain why? And, most importantly, was Kevin Larre right? Should Vincent be suspicious of Lillian?

TWENTY

Vincent endured another sleepless night after reading about Lillian's "suspicious actions" in Kevin Larre's manuscript. He kept looking over at his wife every few minutes wondering about the validity of what he'd read. Under normal circumstances, Vincent would not take to heart anything told to him by anyone until he found out about it for himself. These were not normal circumstances, however. No matter how farfetched and unbelievable his claims were, Kevin Larre had proven to be truthful in his writings.

Snoring came from Lillian's side of the bed, and Vincent was jealous that his wife seemed so relaxed. How could any parent who just found out her daughter was a prostitute sleep so soundly? She certainly didn't seem this peaceful when she was asking him where he'd been all day.

There was a part of Vincent that wasn't so sure about Susan. He knew what he found under her bed was damning evidence that she was selling her body for sex, but that seemed like a vital detail missing from Kevin Larre's manuscript. It was very out of character for Kevin Larre to omit an element of such great consequence. Vincent's doubt about Susan's guilt stemmed not from any trust he had in his daughter, but rather from his trust in what he'd been reading.

Vincent turned on his side facing away from Lillian. The clock next to the bed read 4:37. No one would be up for hours. Lillian worked in the afternoons on Saturdays, and the kids usually slept in like every other teenager in America. He doubted he would see Susan at all this weekend. Her shock and shame were evident when Vincent threw the money and letters on her desk.

Doubting sleep would ever come, Vincent closed his eyes in hopes of getting some kind of peace before tomorrow brought on any new surprises. And, the way things had been going lately, he was sure he could expect some surprises.

Vincent put on a pot of coffee the next morning in hopes of slightly impressing Lillian who was still in bed. He chose not to believe she was doing anything behind his back until he had the proof right in front of him. At least, this way he could still try and have a somewhat normal relationship with his wife.

He reached into his pocket and turned on his cell phone. It was still shut off from yesterday. A minute after he turned it on, a beep told him he had three voicemails. He was sure at least one of them was from Lillian. He punched in his password, and Lillian had actually left two voicemails, both of them asking where he was and when he'd be getting home.

Vincent deleted the first two messages and hoped the third was from Devon with some information regarding Kevin Larre.

He was ready to receive some good news, or at least helpful news. It seemed like every time he tried to gather more information, Vincent was left with more questions than before.

The third message wasn't from Devon, but rather Hank Loreo from the Mercedes dealership. His car was finally ready to be picked up. That would ease some of the tension between him and Neil. At least, he hoped it would since he wouldn't have to borrow his son's car anymore.

Vincent poured two cups of coffee and headed upstairs. He walked into his bedroom where Lillian was still sleeping. He placed one mug on the nightstand next to his wife and sat on the edge of the bed. Lillian woke up after he put the cup down.

"Oh, thank you." Vincent couldn't tell if she sounded confused because she had just woken up or because of his random act of kindness. He hoped it was the former.

"I got a call from the Mercedes people, finally. My car is ready to be picked up. Do you think you can drive me there this morning to pick it up?"

Lillian sat up and reached for her coffee. "Yeah, no problem. I don't work until three." She took a sip from her steaming mug and looked grateful for the hot beverage. "Did they say what was wrong with it?"

"No," Vincent replied. "I don't really care at this point. I just want my car back."

Lillian looked distracted and Vincent immediately thought about the manuscript from Kevin Larre. He hoped he didn't need to be suspicious of his wife's thoughts. Vincent shook his head, knowing he was acting paranoid again. Kevin Larre certainly did a thorough job screwing with Vincent's head.

Vincent went to the bathroom to shower and get ready for the day and whatever revelations it chose to throw at him. If he learned anything over the past week, it was that nothing was ever as calm as it seemed. There was always danger lurking around the corner.

The ride to the dealership was silent—uncomfortably silent. Vincent knew in his heart that this wasn't supposed to be the type of environment created by a husband and wife. Usually, a couple could sit in silence without any tension permeating the air. In the car, it seemed like there was nothing but tension and rigidity.

Vincent looked over at Lillian. He would try to ease the mood by smiling at her if she looked his way. He realized he was expecting too much, however. Lillian's eyes didn't leave the road. It was as if she was purposely avoiding his gaze and any conversation.

When they pulled into the dealership, Vincent was relieved to get out of the tomb-like car. Lillian walked in with him to hear the mechanic rattle off a list of problems that were fixed over the past week. The bill was extravagant, but it was nothing Vincent couldn't handle. Besides, he was in no mood to argue over costs. He'd had a tough week and thought it best to just pay the bill and leave.

"So I'll see you at home, then," said Lillian as they walked out. Vincent noticed how she barely glanced at him. There was definitely something on her mind that she wasn't going to share with him. Even his astute writer's mind couldn't figure out what his wife was thinking.

"Okay. And, maybe we can talk about things when we get home," he said. "I really think we need to figure out what we're going to do about Susan."

"Fine," Lillian replied. She got in her car and drove away before Vincent reached his own car. His drive home was more interesting than his ride there thanks to the idiots he listened to on talk radio. At this point, he'd take any type of discussion, no matter how thoughtless, to counteract the uneasiness surrounding him. Anything to take his mind off of everything that had been plaguing him.

He arrived home a few minutes after Lillian and was fully prepared to finally talk about Susan. This conversation could not be put off any longer. Now was the best time to have it since Lillian wasn't scheduled to work until three.

Lillian was in the kitchen cleaning up from their breakfast that morning.

"Do you need any help with anything?" he asked, trying to open their talk amicably.

"No. There's not that much to take care of." Lillian continued to clean while Vincent took a seat at the kitchen table.

"Is it okay if we talk about Susan now?"

"I guess," Lillian answered, rubbing the back of her hand across her forehead. *You're not the only one who gets a headache from this,* Vincent thought.

"Okay. Well, I think what Patrick suggested…" Vincent's cell phone managed to go off at the most inconvenient time. He got up to walk out of the kitchen. "Hello?" he said into the phone.

"Where the hell are you? You were supposed to be at the signing fifteen minutes ago." Devon sounded extremely agitated. For the first time, Vincent actually forgot to show up to a book signing. "You tell me to treat you like a grownup and not constantly remind you," Devon continued. "Then, you forget to show up the one time I leave you alone."

"I'm sorry," Vincent said. "I've had a lot on my plate lately. I'll get there as soon as possible."

"Do you have a ride?"

"I got my car back this morning."

“Good.” Devon hung up on Vincent, a real switch in their relationship. Vincent was usually the one to hang up on his agent.

Vincent plodded back into the kitchen. “I just got a call from Devon,” he told Lillian. “I completely forgot about a book signing today.”

“Where is it?”

“A bookstore in Ramsey.”

“Fine.” Lillian turned back to her dishes. “Once again, Vincent Kraver chooses work over family.”

Vincent shot her an angry look. “I don’t have time for this. I was supposed to be there fifteen minutes ago.”

“Okay. Sorry. Go on.” Lillian didn’t look the least bit sorry, but Vincent didn’t have time to continue arguing. “What time will you be back?” Lillian called from the kitchen as he headed out the front door.

“You’ll probably be headed out to work by the time I get back.”

“I’ll see you sometime tomorrow I guess.”

Vincent couldn’t think of anything else to say to his wife, so he resolved to just slamming the door.

TWENTY-ONE

Vincent knew Devon would approach him furiously the second he stepped into the bookstore. “How about you wait to yell at me until after the signing?” he suggested.

Devon bit his tongue before he said something inappropriate to Vincent in front of the crowd of fans. “Okay. Just sit down so we can get started.”

Vincent wasn’t used to Devon being so infuriated, but he knew he was justified. He was over forty-five minutes late with no excuse, at least not one that he felt like sharing with his agent. In order to not further irritate Devon, Vincent decided to forgo his usual moment of preparation in the bathroom. He usually couldn’t do a signing without taking a few minutes by himself, but he figured he had enough time in the car on the way here.

Vincent gave a slight nod to Sharla who was sitting in a chair by the entrance waiting for new customers. He walked over to the signing table to begin the long process of mindless chatter with his readers. Before he sat down, however, Vincent assessed the objects on the table: three water bottles, a cup full of Sharpies—and a large yellow envelope with a picture glued to the corner.

“Devon,” he called out, not taking his eyes off the envelope.

"What?"

Vincent ignored the agitation in his agent's voice. "Did you see who dropped that off?" He pointed to the envelope, but Devon didn't bother looking at it.

"No," he replied. "I was busy trying to keep the store owner from losing his shit since you were so late."

"Will you stop flipping out on me? I told you I was sorry." Vincent picked up the envelope and looked at the picture. Lillian and Patrick holding hands in a restaurant. What? His wife and his best friend? They looked happy—like they were on date. "Oh my God."

"What is it?" Devon asked.

Vincent headed into the stacks of books. "I need ten minutes to myself."

Devon's eyes widened. "Are you serious? You're already forty-five minutes late. You can't take time to yourself. What am I supposed to tell the manager?"

"Figure something out!" Vincent yelled, startling some of the customers. He looked around slightly embarrassed by his outburst. "Ten minutes," he said one more time before walking away.

Finding an empty corner of the store, Vincent sat down and opened the envelope to read the next installment of the manuscript by Kevin Larre.

Broken Vows

A week ago, Vincent Kraver was a successful author in the midst of going to book signings to promote his latest novel, *Quiet Thunder.* There was no tension hindering his comfortable lifestyle. There were no secrets keeping him from living a life he'd planned on having ever since college.

It's amazing how much could change in a week. Vincent's life had been altered by someone who he knew nothing about, but this someone obviously knew much about Vincent.

For the first time since earning his success, Vincent felt threatened. He had worked without any reprieve for years to get to where he was today. He was not prepared to have that success questioned or taken away from him. Unfortunately, Kevin Larre had other plans, and Vincent had no other choice but to go with the flow and continue reading.

Vincent didn't think his life could be any more ripped apart after reading about his daughter's sexual entrepreneurship. How could Vincent Kraver have ended up with a daughter who cared nothing about herself or her parents? Didn't she realize how much of an embarrassment it was for Vincent to have failed so miserably at raising his child?

He didn't even know where he went wrong. In his mind, he did everything right. Vincent gave her the clothes she wanted, a house to exceed all comfort levels, and a weekly allowance that made the need for her to earn her own money nonexistent. That obviously didn't stop Susan from trying to make her own money. And apparently, she'd been very successful.

Now there was the new issue with Lillian. After Kevin Larre left him in the dark about his wife's suspicious actions, Vincent felt extremely ill and on edge. He had no idea how to act around Lillian anymore, not that he ever knew how to act around his wife lately. She always seemed suspicious of Vincent's actions, asking where he'd been, demanding to know when he'd be home. Her sudden interest in his schedule was certainly something for Vincent to be wary of.

The amount of stress Vincent was under was most evident when Devon called him to remind him of the book signing he had forgotten. Vincent was never a fan of book signings. His anti-social personality made him an ideal writer except at the events where he actually had to speak to his readers. He always felt he spoke better with his pen than with his voice.

Surprisingly, however, Vincent was glad to go to a book signing. He would gladly welcome anything to take his mind off of his marital problems. Vincent told Lillian he'd be away

for a few hours and quickly left. It felt good to drive to the signing in his Mercedes, and at least something in his life was back to normal.

The line of customers was already out of the bookstore by the time Vincent arrived. From the looks of it, this was going to be a very long book signing. On the up side, he'd be kept busy for several hours feeling bored rather than anxious.

Devon stormed up to Vincent the instant he entered the store. He was noticeably angry at Vincent's tardiness. Vincent responded to his agent's anger with a terse apology and a visit to the restroom. No matter how late he was running, he wasn't going to let his routine be disrupted. He had to prepare himself for hours of socializing with a few moments of complete solitude.

After splashing water on his face and taking a few mind clearing breaths, Vincent was finally ready to face the throng of customers waiting to speak to him and shake his hand. He figured he could take as long as he wanted. He was, after all, the main attraction.

Even after everything he'd been through, there was still a bit of self-centered-ness in the author.

Vincent walked out of the bathroom feeling prepared for the next couple of hours. The sight of the envelope on the

desk, however, took away all the strength he had mustered for the event.

He couldn't handle this. Not another one. When would the manuscripts end? When would the surprises finally be over?

Devon and Sharla were going about with their normal tasks for the book signing. They evidently hadn't noticed anyone unusual drop off the manuscript or they would have told him. Right?

The color drained from Vincent's face and he suddenly felt extremely lightheaded. The room seemed to spin and people's faces blurred together. Could one of the customers be Kevin Larre? Was he watching Vincent panic? Was he smiling at the effect he was having on the great author?

Vincent knew he couldn't sit through a book signing now. He felt like everyone there was out to get him. Everyone there was Kevin Larre.

He walked over to Devon whose anger quickly melted into concern when he saw Vincent's face.

"Oh my God. You look terrible. Are you alright?" The question was rather idiotic. Vincent knew he looked like he was about to pass out. His sudden illness, however, didn't let him respond to Devon with his usual sarcastic wit.

"I need to go home. Make my excuses for me, will you?" Before Vincent could answer, Vincent grabbed the envelope and was out the door.

The drive home was difficult as Vincent tried to avoid swerving off the road. The cold autumn air eased his nausea slightly, but it still wasn't safe for Vincent to be behind the wheel. Vincent didn't care though. He had to get away from the crowd. Kevin Larre was there. He knew it. Kevin Larre was watching him. Taunting him.

The sooner Vincent got home, the sooner he could open the new delivery and read about the next thing that would ruin his life. Vincent relied on the GPS in his car to get him home. He certainly wasn't thinking clearly enough to take himself in the right direction.

After thirty minutes of driving, Vincent finally pulled into his driveway. He was confused by the extra car. Vincent stared at the Jaguar and wondered what Patrick was doing at his house.

Something suddenly clicked in Vincent's head, and his nausea returned even stronger than before. He finally looked at the envelope that was left for him at the signing. The picture in the corner confirmed the unpleasant thought that suddenly filled his head. It was of Lillian and Patrick, at a restaurant together, smiling and holding hands.

TWENTY-TWO

Vincent was fuming. He wondered if smoke could be seen coming out of his ears. The thought of Lillian cheating on him with anyone was enough to send him reeling. But Patrick? His best friend? This was just too unbelievable for Vincent to even consider. Then again, how often had Kevin Larre been wrong?

Even though he'd been right about many of his previous assumptions, Kevin Larre was incorrect about several things in this last manuscript. Most obvious was the fact that Vincent didn't wait to read the delivery. After the last one he'd read, he was very curious to learn about his wife's "suspicious actions." He wouldn't be able to drive for a half an hour with the envelope burning a hole in his passenger seat.

Kevin Larre had also been wrong about Vincent's courtesy towards other people. He had been able to dismiss his ritualistic trip to the restroom before the signing because he was forty-five minutes late. Vincent knew his manners. He was a gentleman, after all. He didn't want to keep his readers waiting any longer than they had been. That is until he spotted the manuscript and found a spot in the corner to read it.

At this point, after receiving so many chapters from Kevin Larre, Vincent knew hoping the information was false would be pointless. Kevin was the one who revealed his daughter's illegitimate actions. What was different about this revelation?

Although, Kevin Larre didn't really reveal anything about his wife. All he did was show a picture of Lillian and Patrick eating dinner together. That didn't mean sex. Patrick may have been holding her hand as a gesture of comfort, not love. Patrick visiting his house didn't automatically mean his wife was having an affair.

There was only one way to find out. Vincent stormed passed Devon on his way to leave the store.

"Where the hell are you going?" his agent asked, running after him.

Not knowing what else to say, Vincent borrowed a line from Kevin Larre's manuscript. "I have to go home. Make my excuses."

Vincent went through a huge array of emotions on his trek home. In the beginning, he was filled with intense anger. He was a great man, a great author and someone whom a great many people admired. How could Lillian have the nerve to cheat on him, especially with Patrick?

When Patrick first came to Morris High, Vincent was the first and only friend Patrick made there. Without Vincent, Patrick would have been miserable. The two people with whom he showed so much love and support, and to whom he had given so much of himself generously over the years, were going behind his back. His wife and his best friend betrayed him. Who could he trust if not Lillian and Patrick?

The anxiety and anger in Vincent kept growing as he got closer to his home. How long had the affair been going on? Did they love each other? He had so many questions that only Patrick and Lillian could answer. If what Kevin Larre wrote was true. Vincent held on to that "if" for dear life.

Vincent hoped that Kevin Larre would be wrong for once. Maybe, he was trying to drive him crazy so he'd lose his cool in front of his fans. Kevin Larre was probably laughing at the great reaction he elicited from his victim. There was no affair—just an elaborate prank set up by a sick and twisted individual.

A red light brought Vincent to a stop. He was still a good twenty minutes from his house, and Vincent began to feel more nervous about what he'd discover. He had a perfect life—at least he thought he did. What would happen to his marriage if he found Lillian in bed with Patrick? Would it end? Or, could it be fixed with counseling?

That question seemed ironic considering his psychologist best friend was the one screwing his wife. A wave of nausea hit Vincent like a sudden avalanche. Vincent lowered his head and gripped the steering wheel as if it would keep him from sinking even further into the hell Kevin Larre was writing about his life.

A bead of sweat rolled down the side of his face as he tried to get a grip on himself. He was probably the only human being who could perspire at the end of November in northern New Jersey.

The honk from the van behind him reminded Vincent where he was. He hit the gas to continue what felt like a trip to death row. For some reason, death row seemed like a welcome alternative to where he was headed now. He knew if Kevin Larre was right, there would be an entirely different kind of death. A much worse kind than merely breathing his final breath.

Maybe him going home to confront Lillian and Patrick wasn't such a great idea. What good could possibly come from it? His marriage would surely end, and his relationship with Neil and Susan would be even more strained. Putting his kids through a divorce would only add to the stress of the situation. Maybe he shouldn't deal with Lillian and Patrick in order to avoid nasty circumstances for his children.

Another thought all of a sudden occurred to Vincent—a thought even scarier than not being able to fix things between him and Lillian. Kevin Larre was clearly intent on sending his manuscripts to Vincent. What if he wasn't the only intended reader?

Vincent couldn't imagine what would happen to his reputation as a respected author if Kevin Larre made it public that his wife was having an affair with his best friend. He spent his entire adult life earning the respect of intelligent readers and critics. Vincent knew everything he had worked for would be lost if this information ever got out to anyone besides himself and Kevin Larre. The image he gave his readers would be smeared along with the future of his career.

Without paying much attention to the road, Vincent finally rounded the corner of his street. For one fleeting moment, he thought Kevin Larre was wrong about the affair in his manuscript. He didn't see Patrick's car in the driveway. As he drove closer, however, he saw the dark blue Jaguar parked close to the garage.

His heart felt like it was beating in his throat. He wasn't ready to face them. Vincent didn't feel he'd ever be ready to confront Lillian and Patrick. His foot eased off the gas and the Mercedes came to a slow roll. After a brief pause in front of his house, Vincent pressed his foot down and continued on down the road. An extra lap around the block seemed like a good idea. Maybe, his life would fix itself if he took a magic spin around the neighborhood.

The second time he drove up to his house, though, didn't change anything. Patrick's car didn't magically disappear. The threat of Lillian having an affair with Patrick was just as great as before. The odds of Vincent walking in and finding his wife and best friend in his bed made his stomach churn.

Vincent pulled into his driveway and parked behind Patrick. At least, Pat wouldn't be able to make a quick getaway with Vincent's Mercedes blocking the way. With envelope in hand, Vincent entered his house.

He closed the door and leaned against it drawing in a few deep breaths. Maybe, Patrick was just paying a friendly visit, stopping by to offer his advice on Susan. Vincent would walk into the kitchen and find Lillian and Patrick sitting at the table, drinking coffee, eating cake, and talking about how to solve the issues in Lillian's and Vincent's lives.

A walk to the kitchen disproved that theory. The emptiness of the room was emphasized by the echo of his footsteps on the cold tiles. Vincent turned around and walked slowly to the stairs. He paused on the first step to see if he could hear anything. A minute of silence passed before he continued climbing the stairs.

His grip on the railing was slippery due to his sweaty palms. Still not ready to face what was probably in the bedroom, Vincent walked to the bathroom. He looked at his reflection in the mirror. Other than looking deathly pale and about to keel over, Vincent thought he was a pretty good looking guy. True, his hair was thinning and he had gained a few pounds since he'd gotten married, but he was in his fifties, and his wife was a distinguished chef.

Vincent thought of Patrick and how well his friend had aged. Patrick managed to keep a full head of hair with wisps of gray that made him look distinguished rather than old. His successful career as a psychologist allowed him to have a yearly gym membership and many vacations to keep up a healthy, youthful appearance. When it came down to it, Patrick probably did have Vincent beat in the looks department. However, that didn't mean Lillian would cheat on him. He may not have been the best looking guy around, but he wasn't hideous either. His wife was still attracted to him, right?

Laughter from his bedroom provided Vincent with a painful answer. The laughter was not his wife's, but rather another man's. Patrick's.

Any nervousness Vincent felt melted away quickly from the heat of his anger. Without wasting any more time, Vincent charged out of the bathroom and into his bedroom.

"Vincent!" Lillian exclaimed. She scrambled to cover her naked body with their five hundred dollar, 900-count Egyptian cotton sheets. "What are you doing home? I thought you were at a book signing for the next few hours."

Vincent watched Patrick move quickly to get his pants on. "Sorry to inconvenience you."

"I-I'm sorry. Vincent, I am *so* sorry." Patrick stuttered the same way he had the previous morning.

"How long has this been going on?" Vincent asked. Lillian and Patrick just looked at each other. "It's a simple question," Vincent continued glaring at Patrick. "How long have you been screwing my wife?"

"Um, I guess about…five months," Patrick answered.

Vincent couldn't believe what he was hearing. "Five months? You've been sneaking around behind my back for five months?"

Lillian began to cry. "I don't know what to say. I'm sorry you had to find out this way."

"Really? How did you want me to find out?"

Vincent's question was answered by silence from the two offenders.

"Is Patrick the early morning errand you had to run yesterday?" Lillian responded with a tiny nod. Patrick didn't say anything. He just stood there looking ashamed.

His friend's odd actions yesterday finally made sense. With Lillian upstairs and Vincent's unexpected drop by, it's no wonder Patrick was on edge.

Vincent was angry, uncomfortable, embarrassed and nauseous, all at the same time. The amount of emotion building up inside him would burst out violently if he didn't leave the room. Vincent spun around and left Lillian and Patrick once again alone in his bedroom. He wondered how many times they'd been alone in there before.

The image of Lillian and Patrick in his bed—arms and legs intertwined, the sweaty, writhing bodies pressed as close and deep as physically possible—made Vincent's head spin. Feeling like he was about to faint, he stumbled down the stairs, gripping tightly to the railing. He tried to make it back to the kitchen for a tall glass of ice cold water. He had been sweating quite profusely due to his natural body chemistry plus the anxiety being created by Lillian and Patrick.

The kitchen, however, proved to be an impossible destination for him to reach. Instead, Vincent locked himself in the bathroom at the bottom of the stairs. He barely leaned over the toilet when his breakfast came up violently. Nothing had ever made him so physically sick before.

What was happening to his life? What had he done to deserve this? From the moment he was born, Vincent Kraver had been forced to live a life of melancholy and solitude, and none of what he went through was remotely his fault. Other people were always responsible for the turbulence in Vincent's life.

Janet Kraver was the worst of everyone. Her constant need to move around from abusive relationship to abusive relationship severely inhibited Vincent's ability to establish any lasting friendships. Even in middle school, when Vincent managed to make his first real friend, his mother had managed to ruin any chances Vincent had at maintaining a permanent relationship with Chris.

Now, the one friend he *had* managed to keep—the one friend he knew to be faithful and trustworthy—had gone behind his back and deceived him in the worst possible way. Patrick had permanently squashed any perception Vincent had of the goodness that existed in other people. Now that his wife and best friend were so obviously false-hearted and deceitful, there was no one in Vincent's life whom he could trust. No one he could turn to when his life was too much to handle on his own.

How had this happened? Vincent lowered the lid of the toilet and sat down. In the course of seven days, his life had been turned completely upside-down. If it wasn't for Kevin Larre, Vincent would still be going about his life the same as before. He wouldn't be reminded of the worst memories from his childhood. He wouldn't be aware of his daughter's illicit affairs. He wouldn't have felt betrayed by Lillian and Patrick. Kevin Larre had certainly accomplished a lot with his manuscripts over the past week.

It was the first time Vincent would have preferred to be blissfully ignorant of his life. The truth was painful, and it wasn't at all what Vincent had pictured his life being. But, Kevin Larre didn't care about Vincent's feelings. Kevin Larre wanted Vincent to realize what kind of life he was truly living.

And, what a miserable life it was. Every chapter Kevin Larre had sent described a part of Vincent's life where he was being let down by people who were supposed to care about him. Kevin Larre's manuscripts pointed out to Vincent that there was no one in his life he could trust. Not his mother. Not his daughter. And, certainly not his wife and best friend.

Footsteps coming down the stairs told Vincent it was time to continue with the unpleasantries. He opened the door and met Lillian and Patrick at the bottom of the stairs.

"So, doctor," Vincent said looking at Patrick, "what would you suggest to solve this family crisis? More therapy?"

"Vincent, we never meant to hurt you," Patrick responded softly.

"What do you mean by that, Patrick? If you didn't want to hurt me, maybe you shouldn't have seduced my wife. Maybe, you shouldn't have gone behind my back and done the most deceitful thing you could think of."

"It's about time you learned to think of someone other than yourself. You've had problems with your marriage long before me and Lillian got together. You were just too self-absorbed to realize it. I'm not the problem here."

"Even if I could wrap my head around that convoluted answer and realize it as a legitimate excuse, you think that would get you off the hook?"

Lillian finally decided to chime in. "You didn't leave me much of a choice, Vincent."

"What are you talking about? You can't possibly try to be blaming any of this on me. I'm not the one who cheated. I would *never* cheat."

"You probably wouldn't be able to find anyone to cheat *with*," Lillian answered. "You're so distracted by your own life that you don't focus on anyone else. You pay almost no attention to me. I can't imagine you being able to pay any attention to another woman."

"My attention is always on you and the kids. I focus on my work in order to make a better life for you."

"Maybe, we better put this conversation off until another time," Patrick said. "None of us can think clearly right now."

"No, I want to have this conversation now. I'm tired of avoiding everything that is wrong in my life." Patrick ignored Vincent and walked out the front door. Vincent followed Patrick out to his car, not willing to let his former friend get away that easily. Lillian stayed behind in the house to answer the phone that started ringing.

"Trust me, Vincent. We can't have a level-headed discussion right now. We need to wait until we've all cooled off a bit."

"Trust you? How can you tell me to trust you?" Patrick opened the door to his Jaguar and climbed in. He made sure to lock the door after he closed it. "You're a coward," Vincent continued. "You're afraid to face me because you know the treachery of what you've done." After what seemed like a fifteen point k-turn, Patrick managed to maneuver his car around Vincent's to get out of the driveway. "Thirty-five years, Patrick! We've been friends for thirty-five years! Fuck you!" Vincent didn't turn to go back into his house until Patrick's Jaguar rounded the corner.

Lillian was off the phone when Vincent walked in. Her face looked ashen and tear stains lined her face. *Good*, Vincent thought. *She should be feeling terrible for what she did.*

"Geez, honey, you look terrible," Vincent said sarcastically.

"Vincent."

"What happened? Were you caught cheating or something?"

Lillian scratched her head, waiting for Vincent's sarcasm to pass. "The emergency room just called. Neil was found unconscious early this morning in a dumpster behind a club. Someone attacked him."

TWENTY-THREE

Vincent had written many scenes that took place in hospital emergency rooms. Nothing quite compared to the real thing, however. The number of patients greatly outnumbered the number of available rooms. There were sick people lining the hallways, either in wheelchairs or on portable beds.

Curtains were used to designate the different "rooms" patients were put in until they were finally admitted to an actual hospital room. The process usually took hours, and someone coming in with a severe injury spent hours in the hallway amid rushing doctors, overtired nurses, and impatient visitors.

Sleep in an emergency room was practically nonexistent. Closed eyelids were no match for the garish overhead lights. Even if the lights were off, the sounds would keep even the heaviest snoozer from falling asleep.

Vincent could hear an old man coughing relentlessly as he walked in the direction of his son's room. Behind another partition, a doctor could be heard explaining to a woman how she had a minor heart attack. There were never any good sounds to be heard in an emergency room. There was crying instead of laughter. Beeping machinery instead of romantic music.

The atmosphere of an emergency room was something even a great author like Vincent Kraver couldn't fully communicate through his writing. The fear he felt about what he'd see when he entered Neil's room was nearly suffocating him.

Lillian didn't look like she was holding up any better. Her intense gaze darted from injured person to injured person, looking for her son. Despite still being angry at her infidelity, Vincent grabbed her hand for support. Lillian looked at him, relieved that he could put aside his animosity for the sake of their son.

Vincent and Lillian turned a corner and saw two police officers standing outside a closed curtain. The parents knew their son occupied the bed on the other side. They slowly approached the officers who looked up when they got nearer.

"Mr. and Mrs. Kraver?" one of the officers asked.

"Yes," Lillian and Vincent answered together.

"I'm Officer Miller and this is Officer Paulson." They flashed their badges before continuing. "Your son was found early this morning in a dumpster outside Utopia. That's the club located near the end of Main Street, by the…"

"I know where it is," Lillian snapped. Her nerves were getting the best of her. Vincent squeezed her hand to calm her down. She responded by pulling her hand away and crossing her arms over her chest.

Vincent felt some rage start to build up deep inside him, but he tempered it because of where they were. He couldn't believe Lillian's attitude toward him. If anyone should be acting agitated and pissed off, it was Vincent. She was the one who cheated on *him,* afterall. He was the one having his life slowly ripped apart by everyone close to him.

"It looks like he was attacked by multiple assailants," said Paulson. "Did you know where he was going last night?"

"He doesn't usually tell us where he's going," said Vincent.

"He doesn't usually tell *you* anything," Lillian scoffed.

Vincent had a strong urge to slap his wife. "Maybe, you can save those comments for later."

"Why? It's true. You and Neil never talk except to argue."

"And, what does that have to do with what happened to him last night? You're blaming the fact that Neil got beat up on me not talking to him?"

"I'm just saying that maybe if you paid more attention to him, he wouldn't be in this situation."

"Folks!" Miller cut them off. "Is it necessary for you two to have this argument now?" Lillian shook her head and looked back at the officers.

"Sorry," Vincent said. "The answer is no. Neither of us knew where he was going last night."

"Do you know who he was with?" Miller asked.

"He usually goes out with his best friend, Justin."

"Does Justin have a last name?"

"Um, Lerner, I think. Justin Lerner?" Vincent looked at Lillian who nodded.

"How come you didn't know where he was going?" asked Paulson with a hint of condescension in his voice.

"I think he's old enough to go out without us shadowing his every move," Lillian answered.

"Apparently not," Paulson retorted. "As you can see, your seventeen-year-old son is in the hospital after you let him go out without knowing where he was going."

Vincent didn't like the accusatory tone of the police officer's voice. "This would have happened whether we knew where he was or not. Don't blame us. We didn't beat up our son."

"You may as well have," said the officer.

"What gives you the right to…"

"Hello?" A weak voice from behind the curtain cut off Lillian's angry reply. Officer Miller pulled the curtain aside to reveal a severely distorted version of Neil Kraver. The entire left side of his face was swollen into one large lump. His eye was completely closed up and his nose was covered with a bloodied bandage. A long gash spread from under the bandage and to his right ear.

"What happened?" Neil asked as he tried to sit up. He gave up after letting out a painful gasp.

"Don't try moving," said Officer Paulson. "You have three broken ribs, a fractured wrist, and two breaks in your right leg. It looks like whoever attacked you used a bat or some other blunt object." Lillian cringed when the officer described his injuries.

"I was attacked?" Neil looked confused, which wasn't surprising considering how many hits to the head he must have taken.

"Do you remember anything about last night?" Officer Miller asked. "Anything at all? Who you went out with? Where you went? Who you may have met?"

"I went to Utopia in Morristown with Justin," Neil said, looking at Lillian.

"Who else was there?" she asked.

"I don't know. A lot of people go there on Friday nights."

"Did you see anyone suspicious while you were there? Maybe someone watching you?"

Neil thought hard about the previous night and tried to remember anything about his attack. It was difficult to tell how much he was recollecting because the bloating in his face kept him from forming any kind of expression.

"How about you describe what you did last night step by step," Vincent suggested. He hoped his experience writing crime novels would aid in discovering what happened to his son. Neil looked at the two police officers who nodded their agreement to Vincent's proposal.

"I drove over to Justin's house around six," Neil began. "We ordered some pizza and hung out with Christina and Diane. They're just some girls from school. About nine o'clock, Justin and I went with the girls to Utopia."

"How'd you get in?" Paulson asked. "I thought it was an eighteen and over place."

"It is, but I look eighteen and I have some buddies who work there." This comment raised some eyebrows among the adults, but no one chose to comment.

"Anyway, we were hanging out with some random people we met there. I don't remember their names. We always meet random people wherever we go. At some point, we went out for some cigarettes—Justin and me. I actually remember pointing out a weird guy who was outside. It was after eleven and the guy was wearing sunglasses. I thought that was kind of strange."

"Do you remember what else he was wearing?" Paulson poised his pen over his notepad preparing to take notes.

“Nothing special. Black pants, black long sleeved shirt, black boots. Even his hair was black. Kind of shaggy, covering part of his face.”

Vincent’s body stiffened upon hearing Neil’s description of the stranger he saw at the club. Looking around, it didn’t seem like anyone else was aware of his intense reaction. They were too focused on Neil.

“How tall was he?” Paulson continued his questions.

“Probably about my height.”

“Excuse me,” Vincent said. He left his son and wife with the police officers to gather his wandering thoughts. His search for privacy, however, proved unsuccessful on his journey through the hallways. Beds provided an unpleasant border with victims suffering various degrees of injuries. Respirators kept many of the elderly patients from expiring in the public spaces of the emergency room.

A child’s scream could be heard in the distance. Vincent wondered what was causing the little girl such tremendous pain. He spotted a woman sitting in a chair with her face covered in bruises. It was probably the result of disobeying the burly man sitting next to her, but that wouldn’t be the story the doctor would hear. The doctor would most likely be told she fell down the stairs, an accident she’s had several times within the past few months.

Vincent eventually reached a less populated area of the emergency room. He approached a wall lined with vending machines. Reaching into his pocket, Vincent pulled out a dollar bill and stuck it into of the snack machines. He stared at the food choices wondering what he wanted.

What were the chances the man who attacked Neil was the same man sending him stories of his life? Was Kevin Larre responsible for putting his son in the emergency room? Thus far, Kevin Larre had not shown any sign of violence. His actions were eerie and intimidating, but certainly not violent. An attack, especially one as brutal as the one on Neil, was completely out of character for the mysterious author. Besides, the police officers said it looked like Neil was attacked by more than one person. The more Vincent thought about it, the more unlikely it seemed that the peculiar manuscript writer and his son's attacker were one and the same.

There was still a twinge in Vincent's chest that he usually felt when something wasn't making sense. His strong disbelief in coincidences made Vincent think everything he went through this week was directly related to his son's assault. It was especially alarming that Neil saw a man exactly like the one who had been stalking him at his book signings.

Stalking. Was the dark stranger actually stalking Vincent? He had only shown up to two of his signings. Or rather, Vincent had only *noticed* him at two of the signings. It was probably the dark stranger who was the one who left the manuscript at the last event even though Vincent himself didn't see him there.

There were so many things that didn't make sense. Vincent knew he was sharper than most, and he felt extremely disturbed by the perplexity Kevin Larre was putting him through.

"There you are." Lillian came up behind him along with the two police officers. "Why did you leave?"

Vincent looked from his wife, to Officer Miller and Officer Paulson, and back to the vending machine. He didn't know how much time had passed since he put his dollar in. "I thought I was hungry," he lied. "I guess I'm not." He hit the change return button and heard four quarters clang in the machine. He reached down to collect his change before turning to face the other three. "What?"

The looks on Lillian and the officers' faces were of utter bafflement. Lillian was the first to respond. "You left your son's bedside because you thought you were hungry? Are you ever not thinking about yourself?"

"I had to think some things over, about Neil and what happened. And, I needed some quiet."

"What were you thinking about?" asked Miller.

Vincent responded with another question. "Was Neil able to identify who the guy in black was?"

"No," Paulson replied. "And, he has no idea who attacked him. He said he doesn't have any enemies. And, your wife said you guys don't have any enemies either." Vincent looked down knowing he had to tell the officers about Kevin Larre. Paulson noticed his uncomfortable body language. "Is that true?" he asked.

Looking unsteadily back and forth between his wife and the police officers, Vincent answered slowly. "Not entirely."

Lillian shifted her weight from one leg to the other. "What do you mean?"

"Last Sunday at my book signing in Ridgewood, a guy wearing all black and dark sunglasses came up to me when it was over. He said he was my biggest fan but he didn't want my autograph. He was definitely disturbing, but I didn't think much of it. Then, he showed up at another signing, and I'm pretty sure he stopped by the assisted-living facility where my mother lives when I was visiting her."

"What's the name of that facility?" asked Miller.

"Everly."

"Wait," said Lillian, looking confused. "When did you visit your mother?"

"Wednesday night. The night you went out to get drinks with Franci. Well, that's what you *said*, anyway."

The police officers listened without questioning the couple. Lillian pursed her lips together giving away that Vincent was right in assuming she had been with Patrick that night. "Is there anything else?" she asked.

"Yeah," Vincent said facing the policemen. "I've been getting manuscripts from a guy named Kevin Larre. They're about me. Really accurate details of personal events in my life. I'm not sure if the guy in black and Kevin Larre are the same person."

"Do you feel threatened?" asked Paulson.

Vincent braced himself before answering. He knew Lillian's reaction would be no less than atomically explosive.

"I'd say so. He managed to leave a few deliveries in my son's car when I borrowed it to get to the signing on Wednesday, and in my office at home."

Officer Miller paused in his note taking. "He broke into your son's car and into your house?" Vincent nodded and avoided looking at Lillian. Nothing, however, could protect him from hearing her rage.

"Wait a minute. Let me make sure I'm hearing this right. This man has been sending you crazy mail, broke into Neil's car, and broke into our house? And, you kept this from me? How could you keep a secret like that? You should have told me from the very beginning! And, the police! This isn't something you keep to yourself!"

"Well, it looks like we've both been keeping dark secrets from each other," Vincent countered.

Lillian's eyes nearly doubled in size. "Don't you dare compare my secret with yours. Our son was nearly killed last night because you were too idiotic to report an obviously dangerous stalker!"

"Can you please lower your voice?" Officer Miller did his best to calm down Lillian. His attempts were futile.

"Look," said Vincent. "He's never done anything violent before. I didn't know this would happen."

"Well, now you know," Lillian said raising her arm. Officer Paulson grabbed her wrist before she could take a swing at Vincent.

"Okay, let's separate you two for a while." Officer Paulson started to pull Lillian out of the waiting area.

"Let go of me," she said. "I'm not gonna waste my energy on him."

"Maybe you shouldn't stay together tonight." Officer Miller stood between the dueling spouses.

"No problem," Lillian responded. "I have another place I can stay. I just need to make a call." Pulling out her cell phone, she headed for the exit.

"Tell Patrick I said hi," Vincent called out to her as she stormed off.

"Dude, this sucks." Justin sat next to Neil's hospital bed. "I actually had to take the bus to school today."

"So sorry to inconvenience you," Neil replied.

Justin smirked. "You better be sorry. You ruined my already crappy Monday."

"I don't think I'll be back at school for at least another week. And, I certainly won't be driving."

"Well, in case I haven't said it enough yet, you suck." Neil laughed at his friend's sarcastic humor. It was a relief to see him after two days of doctors and nurses who feigned concern for his condition.

"Hey Neil," said Vincent walking into the room.

"Hi, Mr. Kraver!" exclaimed Justin with a big cheesy smile.

"Justin, would you mind giving me and Neil some privacy?" He pulled a couple of dollars from his pocket. "Here, get yourself a treat."

"Gee, thanks Dad!" Justin grabbed the money from Vincent and hustled out of the room. Vincent took Justin's seat next to Neil's bed.

"How are you feeling?" Vincent asked.

"A little better."

After a brief pause, Vincent continued. “Look, I want to say something to you that’s really hard since I don’t do it often. So, just bear with me.”

“Okay.”

“I want to apologize.”

Neil tilted his head like a confused puppy. “For what?”

“For everything. I haven’t exactly been the most caring father I could be. And, I just want you to know that things will be different from now on. I really only ever wanted the best for you. I never expected this to happen.”

“Dad, it’s not like this is your fault.”

Vincent thought it best to not tell Neil about how he’d kept the secrets of the manuscript and Kevin Larre from the police. “Just know that I love you, and I’ll try to take better care of you in the future.”

Neil nodded. “Thanks, that means a lot.” The father and son stared at each other in silence for thirty seconds. “Well…I think I’m gonna get some sleep. I’m still kind of hazy from the drugs they’ve been giving me.”

“Okay,” Vincent said. “I’ll be back later.”

Neil turned over onto his side facing away from Vincent and closed his eyes. Vincent felt a real accomplishment after his apology and was hopeful of fixing his relationship with Neil.

As he went to get up from the chair, he saw Justin's backpack on the floor by the door. The zipper was slightly open, and Vincent paused on his way out when something in the bag caught his eye. It looked like black hair was sticking out from the backpack. Looking around to make sure no one was watching, Vincent leaned over and peered further into the bag. His jaw dropped when he saw the contents: a black wig, black clothes, sunglasses, and, worst of all, another yellow envelope.

TWENTY-FOUR

Vincent couldn't believe his eyes. It was the most unbelievable solution to the mystery. Justin Lerner, Neil's idiot best friend, was the dark stranger at the book signings? Justin was the one who broke into Neil's car and his house? Justin was Kevin Larre?

The idea was ridiculous. Justin could barely tie his shoes every morning let alone pull off a prank like this. It was even more ludicrous to think Justin was capable of writing the manuscripts. Insane. Unbelievable!

Before letting another second slip by, Vincent removed his jacket and wrapped it around the backpack. He made sure Neil was still facing the other way when he scooped up the startling evidence and snuck out of the room. He looked down the hall and saw Justin conversing with a nurse. His body language indicated he was putting on the charm. It took all his inner strength for Vincent not to rush over to him and throw him to the ground after causing so much damage to his life. Irreparable damage.

Vincent walked quickly out of the hospital and to his car. His energy was soaring. The mystery was finally over, even if the outcome was an extreme disappointment. He kept the backpack hidden in his jacket until he was a few blocks from the hospital.

After driving for a few minutes, Vincent pulled into the parking lot of a gas station. He unwrapped Justin's bag and sifted through it to make sure his eyes weren't playing tricks on him in the hospital.

But, his eyes portrayed the truth. There was the black shaggy wig that covered half of Justin's face when he wore it. The black clothes and boots were the same that the dark stranger wore when Vincent encountered him at his book signings. And, the large sunglasses were the final touch to Justin's perfect disguise.

The most unbelievable part of this revelation was definitely the fact that Justin must have been Neil's attacker. Justin and Neil had been best friends for almost six years. He may have been an asshole to many people, including Vincent, but Justin had always been loyal to Neil.

Vincent couldn't begin to figure out the motivation behind Justin's actions. His reasons for everything would remain a mystery until he confessed. The task of getting one of those out of Justin would be left to the police.

He was about to close the evidence bag when another thought occurred to Vincent. He knew it was a mistake, but his curiosity blocked out all other reasoning. Grabbing the envelope out of the bag, Vincent tucked the next chapter of the manuscript underneath the passenger seat. He then zipped up the backpack and headed for the police station.

Lillian hadn't been home in two days, and Vincent refused to call Patrick's house looking for her. She would find out soon enough from the police that Justin was the culprit. He was the mastermind behind the manuscript that ultimately destroyed his family. He hoped the police pointed out to her that Vincent was the one who solved the case.

The idea of Justin being the clever, mysterious author actually made Vincent chuckle. His chuckle turned into full blown laughter. Vincent was definitely losing it. He was in desperate need of sleep.

The past two nights were relatively restless for him. Sleep was hard for Vincent to come by when his mind was occupied with everything that had transpired over the past nine days. Susan still hadn't come home after the night he and Lillian confronted her, not that he blamed her. After being accused of prostitution, there was a slim chance that his daughter would show her face in the house any time soon.

Vincent's marriage was most definitely over, as was his friendship with Patrick. It was a real shock when he discovered their affair, and Justin was the one to thank. How had a seventeen-year-old moron been able to wreak so much havoc on Vincent and his family?

The answer to the question couldn't be answered. Vincent truly had no idea. It was rare that he found himself in a position of not knowing, but hopefully that was now coming to an end. The police would use the evidence Vincent delivered earlier that day to get Justin to confess to his crimes. Vincent knew he'd confess. There was no getting around the evidence that Vincent found in his backpack.

There was, of course, the one piece of evidence that Vincent chose not to turn in. In fact, he just remembered he left it under the passenger seat of his car. He looked at his watch and saw it was past eleven. Vincent decided to wait until the morning to get the manuscript. He could wait to read it at a later time. It's not like he'd be receiving any more deliveries from Kevin Larre.

Vincent walked into his bedroom to change into his pajamas. He brushed his teeth with extra vigor and even ran a comb through the white fuzz on his head. Nothing could kill his high spirits tonight. Kevin Larre was caught. The mystery was solved, thanks to Vincent Kraver.

As he crawled into bed, Vincent looked forward to finally getting a full night's rest. He laughed again when he thought of Justin as being the genius behind everything. With a shake of his head, Vincent drifted peacefully off to sleep.

TWENTY-FIVE

The next morning, Vincent made himself coffee and a bacon cheese omelet. With Lillian gone, he didn't have to hear about how his diet would eventually kill him. He opened the fridge and took out his low-fat, lactose-free milk to pour in his coffee.

The house was unusually quiet and peaceful. That wouldn't last long since Neil would be coming home today. Lillian offered to drive him home. It would be the first time Vincent saw his wife in three days. He wondered how awkward it would be not only for them, but also for Neil. Vincent and Lillian would need to make their divorce as painless as possible for the kids. Well, more so for Neil. After all, who knew when they'd see Susan again?

The phone rang as Vincent washed his dishes. After drying off his hands, Vincent answered it.

"Good morning, Mr. Kraver. This is Officer Miller."

"Good morning," Vincent replied. "How are you?"

"Things have been busy here at the station," the officer replied. "We've been talking to Justin for several hours."

"And, how's that going?"

"It hasn't really been going anywhere. He's been very tight-lipped."

"Really? Isn't it your job to get criminals to talk?"

"He says he won't talk to anyone except you."

Vincent was puzzled by this information. "Me? What does he want to talk to me for?"

"I don't know," Miller answered. "But, one thing he keeps saying is he's definitely *not* Kevin Larre."

At the moment, Vincent wanted nothing more than for this mystery to be over. And, he thought it was. He thought he had it all figured out. Even if the idea of Justin being Kevin Larre was completely outlandish, at least it brought the problem to a close. Now, just when Vincent was starting to relax, Justin had to go and reopen the entire situation by claiming not to be the enigmatic author.

The last envelope that Vincent had taken out of Justin's bag the night before still sat under the front seat of his car. He wondered if he should bring it in with him into the police station. It was, after all, evidence that Vincent decided to take for himself rather than have the police get their hands on it. If the police had taken it, who knows when Vincent would have been able to read it? Who knows if he would *ever* be allowed to read it?

Vincent thought about the other manuscripts he had received over the past week. He kept them stored in the same drawer as his journals, locked away from everyone except himself. They were locked away from Kevin Larre as well, considering he was able to break into his office and desk drawer on a previous occasion. Those manuscripts would remain where they were. The police didn't seem overly concerned about them, especially since they caught their obvious deliverer.

As long as they didn't ask for them, Vincent would keep the manuscripts for himself, including the one he had yet to read. Even after the other chapters brought out the worst aspects of Vincent's past and present, he was still interested in finding out what was written in the next one.

He wondered if that was due to his curiosity or his narcissism. Vincent hoped it was the former. As a writer, he was bound to be a little bit curious, right?

Vincent entered the police station, leaving the manuscript in its spot under the seat. He was led down a number of hallways until Officer Miller came to greet him.

"Good morning, Mr. Kraver."

"Good morning. At least it was until you called."

Officer Miller nodded his head. "Yeah. Most people don't like getting calls from police officers no matter what time of day it is."

"So," Vincent said rubbing his hands together. "Justin said he wants to talk to me? Where is the little prick?"

"Follow me," Miller replied. The policeman silently led Vincent down another maze of hallways. He stopped at an open door to a room that contained a single wooden table with a chair on either side of it. "You can take a seat in there," Miller said, gesturing towards the room. "I'll go get Justin."

Vincent took a seat at one end of the table. A quick survey around the room showed nothing elaborate. There was a door on the wall opposite to where he came in, along with a big one-way mirror. He wondered if Officers Miller and Paulson would be watching Justin and Vincent when they spoke. It would be extremely naïve to think they'd have complete privacy during their talk.

Less than a minute passed before Officer Miller led Justin into the room. His hands were bound by handcuffs and he sported blue prison garb. It was quite a difference from his usual baggy jeans and tight tee-shirts. He was also forced to forfeit the backwards cap that normally covered his greasy hair.

Despite his current location, Justin seemed to be in high spirits. Did this kid ever get upset about anything? If he wasn't mistaken, Vincent thought Justin might actually be enjoying his time behind bars.

"How are you on this fine morning, Mr. Kraver?" Yes, Justin was definitely taking pleasure in his situation, though Vincent could not even begin to understand why.

"Not as good as you apparently. Blue seems to be your color."

"It's definitely not black today, right? They took that outfit away from me."

Justin walked over to sit down opposite Vincent. After making sure they were situated, Officer Miller left the room, giving the two of them complete privacy, save for the one-way mirror.

"So," said Vincent. "I'm not sure of the proper etiquette in this type of situation. Should I call you Justin? Or do you prefer Kevin?"

"Why would you call me Kevin?" Justin asked. "Didn't the police guys tell you that I'm not Kevin Larre?"

"They mentioned you denied it. I'm not sure how convinced I am."

"Believe me, I wish I was Kevin. The guy is crazy smart. I barely passed my gym class." Justin scratched his head in a way that seemed to emphasize his mindlessness.

"Okay, if you aren't Kevin Larre, why don't you tell me who he is? The floor is yours." Vincent leaned back in his seat to give Justin a chance to finally explain the missing piece of the puzzle.

"Actually," said Justin, "I was given specific orders to *not* tell you who he is. He kind of doesn't want to get caught, you know?'

"And, I'm just supposed to believe you?"

"Uh, yeah." Justin plastered on his usual cheesy smile. Vincent resisted the urge to reach over and punch the smile off his face.

Vincent leaned forward and crossed his arms on the table. "If you're not going to tell me who Kevin Larre is, then perhaps you can tell me how you know him, and why you're acting as his delivery boy."

Justin mirrored Vincent's posture before answering. "That's simple enough. He's been paying me. I could always use a little extra money."

"How much has he been paying you?"

"A hundred dollars per delivery. Plus a little extra for my friends when we had to attack Neil."

Vincent felt the blood drain from his face. "Who is he? Tell me who Kevin Larre is."

"Sorry, man. No can do. But, I'm guessing you'll find out soon enough on your own."

"Really?" said Vincent. "Why is that?"

"You haven't read the last manuscript yet, have you?" Vincent looked at Justin blankly, a total giveaway that his assumption was correct. Justin laughed at his reaction. "Wow, I really wish I was half as perceptive as Kevin. That guy knows you well. He said you probably wouldn't be in a rush to read this one."

Vincent got up from the table and headed to the door. "I'm not gonna listen to any more of this. You made your point. I have other important places to be."

"That's true," Justin replied. "I heard Neil is coming home from the hospital today. Tell him I said hi and that I'm sorry, but money sometimes rules out over friendship."

Vincent exited the room before giving Justin a chance to say anything else. He walked quickly to avoid bumping into Officer Miller. He was certainly not in the mood to explain how he kept the latest manuscript for himself.

Hopping into his car, Vincent drove speedily out of the parking lot in the direction of the hospital. After his visit to the police station, Vincent wasn't sure what disturbed him more—Justin's committed denial of being Kevin Larre, or the fact that Vincent actually believed him.

Vincent arrived home from the hospital a few hours later, and trudged into his house. He didn't forget the envelope in the car this time. He dreaded reading it, but he knew it was bound to happen sooner or later. He went to unlock his office for some privacy while he read.

Lillian would be home in a few minutes with Neil. The parents had met in the hospital to fill out the necessary paperwork to discharge their son. Lillian agreed to drive Neil home since she had to get some things before heading off to work that day.

Vincent had just shut the door to his office when he heard the front door open. He sat listening to them move through the house. Lillian walked to the kitchen while Neil made his way slowly up the stairs to his bedroom. After a few minutes, he heard silence and assumed Lillian had left for work. Shuffling outside his office door, however, told him otherwise.

Wondering what Lillian was doing outside his office, Vincent walked to the door and opened it. The hallway was empty, but the table where he usually retrieved his mail had a plate of cookies along with a note.

Dear Vincent,

I know things have been strained with us lately, but you are still the man I fell in love with all those years ago. We have two children together, and we owe it to them to try and make things work. For what it's worth, I am truly sorry for any pain I have caused you over the past few months. I'll be at work until midnight tonight, but I would love it if we could sit down and talk calmly together tomorrow.

Still with love,

Lillian

This was certainly a shock. Was it true? Did Lillian actually hope to reconcile their differences? The note seemed genuine. Hoping for the best, Vincent popped a cookie in his mouth. No matter what happened, Lillian would always be able to win him back through his stomach. Of course, it may take more than cookies for him to forgive her for what she did with Patrick.

Vincent returned to his office and closed the door. He didn't bother locking it in case Neil needed him for anything. He brought the plate of cookies to his desk and ate another one before opening the envelope he found in Justin's backpack. The picture glued to the corner was the portrait of Vincent that appeared on the back covers of his books.

Vincent flipped the switch of his fireplace before taking a seat at his desk. He opened the envelope, and once again, began to read another chapter of his life written by Kevin Larre, an author whom he still had no idea of his true identity.

TWENTY-SIX

Almost Over

The past couple of days went by in a blur for Vincent. With so many events transpiring, getting a grip on things was an impossible task. Vincent knew the life he led a week and a half ago was over. He no longer knew his wife. He no longer had any understanding of his children. It seemed like his family had been completely ripped apart, and Vincent was powerless to fix any of it.

He pulled into the driveway of the house he thought was perfect, just like the rest of his life. Now, he felt nothing but anxiety and tension. With a heavy heart, Vincent walked into the "mansion." Lillian and Neil would be home in a few minutes. They all left the hospital at around the same time.

Heading to his office, Vincent wanted to get some peace and quiet before his family arrived home. He closed the door in time to hear the front door open and Lillian help Neil up the stairs to his bedroom. He wondered where Susan was and if she was planning on coming home. She hadn't been home in days.

After about ten minutes of solitude in his office, Vincent decided to go upstairs and check on Neil. He was surprised to find a plate of cookies with a note on top of it from Lillian. It

was an apology note asking if they could talk when she got home from work that night. Vincent picked up the cookies and the note with a feeling of slight relief and hope. Maybe, after everything that had been going on lately, he and Lillian would finally be able to reconcile.

He returned to his office with mixed feelings about what he'd discovered over the past week. Eating a few of his wife's cookies, Vincent sat down at his desk to read the latest manuscript from Kevin Larre.

He didn't know how he should be feeling. On the one hand, he should be feeling relieved as he finally knew who the mysterious dark stranger was. It was hard to believe that Justin, Neil's friend who couldn't seem to pass any of his classes without his parents shelling out a hefty sum of money, had been able to take advantage of a man like Vincent Kraver. Still, it was pointless to argue the facts.

There was also relief for Vincent in knowing Neil was finally home. After a severe beating in an alley behind a club, Neil had spent a few days in the hospital recovering from his injuries. Vincent had made sure to visit Neil as often as he could in the hospital in an attempt to heal their rocky relationship. While Neil's injuries from his attack would take several weeks to disappear, Vincent was sure the breaks, fractures, and bruises of their relationship would take much longer to mend.

Knowing Justin was behind bars was yet another reason for Vincent to finally relax. However, the man still found himself on edge. Just because Justin was locked up didn't mean Kevin Larre would go away. He would find another person, another delivery boy, to get his manuscripts to Vincent until his story was finished. When would he be finished? Vincent still didn't have a clue.

As Vincent read the latest manuscript from Kevin Larre, he felt his throat start to tighten. It must have been the nerves and stress he had undergone over the past ten days. After all, what had he learned about his family in such a short amount of time? His wife, the ambitious chef he'd fallen in love with because of how unlike his mother she was, was sleeping with Patrick Donway, Vincent's best and only real friend since high school, and a psychologist whom Vincent turned to any time he needed advice. God, he felt like such an idiot knowing now that he probably complained about Lillian to the man who held her in his arms mere hours later.

His throat constricted even more when he remembered what he'd learned about Susan. His daughter claimed she never slept with anyone for money, but once again, it was pointless to argue the facts. He and Lillian had found the photos, had found the letters, and worst of all, had found the money. It was a painful revelation that he would not very quickly, if ever, get over.

At least, he hadn't discovered anything new about Neil. It was obvious Vincent had some issues to work through with his son, but there was nothing surprising about that. In fact, it was rather shocking that Neil was the only one in his life who he was sure kept no secrets from him.

"That's the case, so far," Vincent thought to himself. What if the delivery of another manuscript once again threw Vincent's life into a dangerous spin? How many more surprises could Vincent handle before completely losing it?

Vincent reached up and loosened the collar of his shirt which seemed to be strangling him. Why was he having so much trouble breathing? He stood up from his desk to lower the thermostat, but as he rose, he noticed something in the manuscript that he hadn't seen before. His eyes widened and his mouth dropped open when he realized how naïve he had been.

He knew who Kevin Larre was. It was staring him in the face the entire time, and he'd been too dense to notice. Any good mystery writer would have figured it out right away. Shock would be an understatement for what Vincent felt when he realized how stupid he was.

Vincent looked at the name Kevin Larre. He closed his eyes and saw the name in his head. As if he was hallucinating, the letters of Kevin Larre's name rearranged themselves to

reveal a new name—a name that Vincent Kraver knew all too well.

Right in front of his eyes, K-E-V-I-N L-A-R-R-E became N-E-I-L K-R-A-V-E-R.

The End

Note to Father: Now that you know who I am, I hope you appreciate the effort I put forth in making this mystery for you. I really hope you're enjoying the cookies I made for you as well…

The manuscript fell out of Vincent's hands. Pages scattered on the desk, some falling to the floor. It couldn't be. The tightening of his throat proved the horrible situation was happening for real.

There were peanuts in the cookies. Cookies that were made by his son, not his wife. It made no sense. Why would Neil kill his father? It made no sense. Did it?

Vincent opened the second drawer down on the right side of his desk. Pushing aside the clutter of pens and notepads, he found what he was looking for—his Epipen, his lifeline. It was then that he remembered, however, that he didn't have any medicine with which to fill the syringe. Of all the things Lillian had nagged him to do over the past several months, refilling his epinephrine was something to which he probably should have listened.

For the first time in his life, Vincent was scared--truly scared. He didn't want to die. He looked around at everything in his office, everything he had worked so hard for. In a few minutes, none of it would matter.

Vincent stumbled over to his leather armchair. The leather used to feel good against his hot skin. Now, it provided no comfort. All it could do was soak up the life that was quickly leaking out of him.

Rapidly reaching for the phone on the table next to him, Vincent accidentally knocked it to the floor along with the lamp. Together, they made a thundering crash that could easily be heard throughout the entire house. Vincent didn't know why he reached for the phone. The tightness in his throat kept him from being able to speak. Still, he bent down to press 9-1-1 just in case the police would be able to make it to his house in time.

Now *there* was something that made no sense. In time for what? To see him die? That was a comforting thought.

Vincent fell to the floor and was about to dial when his office door swung open. Moving slowly, having just gotten home from the hospital, Neil Kraver came into the room.

"Hey, dad. Boy, you don't look so good." Neil looked around the room at the half-eaten plate of cookies, the pile of papers on the floor, and his father sprawled on the floor next to the phone and a broken lamp. "I heard a loud crash and thought I'd come down here to make sure everything was okay. Are you okay?"

Vincent didn't have the ability to speak, but he knew if he did, he would be speechless. After discovering the secrets of his wife and daughter, he had hoped it would all be over. Unfortunately, Neil had the biggest secret of all, a secret he was finally ready to share with his father.

Neil walked over to his father's desk and took a cookie off the plate. Popping the treat into his mouth, he grinned broadly.

"That's pretty good. Not bad for a first attempt, right? Baking isn't exactly one of my strong points."

Neil continued his slow journey around the room. He admired the bookshelves and stopped on the row of novels written by Vincent Kraver. "Wow," he said, pointing to the collection. "That's a lot of books. You must be famous or something."

Walking with a slight limp, Neil made his way toward Vincent. He stepped over his father who was still lying on the floor and took a seat on the big leather armchair.

"You don't mind if I sit here, do you? I've had a rough couple of days."

Vincent shook his head and his throat continued to tighten.

After looking around the room, Neil finally settled his gaze on Vincent. "You have a nice office. I've only been in here a couple of times, but I never really looked around."

Vincent already knew his son had broken into his office, as well as his drawer with the journals. He must have somehow discovered where he kept the spare keys.

"It's about time you invited me in here. You always seem to be busy with your writing and making yourself look better. Work always came first with you." If Vincent wasn't mistaken, tears welled up in Neil's eyes. They quickly dried up when Neil glanced briefly away from his father.

"I'm your son," Neil continued, now looking directly at Vincent. "It took a severe beating in an alley behind a club for you to realize that I was in your life. Of course, you were always on my case about getting into a good college, keeping my grades up, making sure I wrote my admissions essays. I always asked myself when you walked away whether you were concerned about me and *my* life, or the way I made *you* look. Because, God forbid Vincent Kraver's son would not get into Princeton. How bad would that look for you?"

Neil paused briefly to catch his breath. His injuries would take a while to heal. "This really is a nice office. You're probably wondering how I found the spare keys you had so cleverly hidden? Am I right?"

Vincent nodded.

"Well," Neil continued, "this may surprise you, but I've read all of your books. Seriously, I think they're great. I'm a huge fan." Neil took a short pause, dramatically letting out a large exhale. He was clearly enjoying himself.

"Unfortunately, for you, one of your favorite spots to hide clues in your books is behind picture frames. That gets old after a while. Maybe, you should think of something new for your next book. Anyway, since I knew you must keep a spare key to your office, I decided to wake up early one day, hide your keys from you, cut school, and see where you went all day. Pretty smart, right? That shouldn't be too surprising though since I'm Vincent Kraver's son.

Nod.

"Anyway, when you walked into the room in the house that no one ever goes in, I figured the key was somewhere in there. And, your books made you completely predictable with the picture frame. No offense."

Vincent didn't know what else to do, so he just continued staring up at Neil.

"Now, I love pranks, so once I found your journals, I knew exactly what I wanted to do with them. I had to think of a pseudonym though, and all I could come up with was Kevin Larre. Was that a good name?"

Nod.

"I thought so too. I told Justin about my plan, and he thought it was hilarious. He really wanted to be a part of it. I'm a nice guy, so I let him. He went out and got the black wig, black clothes, and sunglasses. That's the great thing about Justin. Once he gets excited about something, he goes all out. We'll be laughing about this once he's out of jail in a few years. He told the police that I paid him, right? Or rather, Kevin Larre paid him."

Vincent nodded again since there was nothing else he could do.

"Hmm. I wonder why he said that. I only gave him cab money when he had to leave school to drop off some manuscripts. I wonder if he's expecting me to pay him. I don't think I'd really have the money to pay him. I mean, I practically emptied my savings when I planted that money under Susan's bed."

The shock on Vincent's face must have been obvious.

"You actually thought Susan was selling herself?" Neil asked.

Nod.

"God, I don't know what guy in his right mind would pay to get any of that. Of course, some guys have weird tastes. No, Justin just asked me to do that as a favor to him. He'd get so pissed whenever Susan would ignore his sexual advances, even though she made it with practically every other guy in school. So, we just wrote some letters and took out the money and left it with the pictures for fun. It made Justin feel better, and I don't really give a shit about Susan anyway."

Everything Neil was revealing now was like a knife through Vincent's heart. He knew if Neil hadn't told him about Susan, he would have gone to the grave thinking his daughter was a prostitute. He wanted now, more than anything, to be able to tell Susan he knew the truth, and that he loved her despite her relationships with the boys in her school.

He also wanted to tell Lillian of their daughter's innocence. Vincent was horrified to think of the relationship that would now exist between Lillian and Susan, all because of a prank pulled by Neil and his best friend.

Vincent's throat was almost completely closed up now, and his breathing was getting more and more strained. Pretty soon, his breathing would completely stop, and there was nothing he could do about it.

"I can't believe you never found out about mom and Patrick," Neil continued. "I actually felt kind of bad for you. You really thought mom and Franci went out drinking after midnight? You can be surprisingly dense for a writer sometimes. I wrote that part of the manuscript as a favor to you. I figured someone should clue you in."

There was now no air going into Vincent's lungs. His throat was completely swelled shut. Only minutes were left of Vincent's life. He reached for his throat and let his head fall onto the carpet.

"Okay," Neil said, "it looks like I'm losing your attention, so I'll just cut to the chase. You probably want to know why I decided to send you the manuscripts and make your life a living hell. Right?"

Nod.

Neil edged himself off the chair and sat on the floor next to his father. It was the only way to make sure Vincent looked at him when he spoke.

"College."

College?

"Yes." Neil nodded. "College. You wanted me to go to Princeton, or Yale, or Dartmouth, or Cornell."

Vincent wouldn't know how to respond even if he could speak. What was Neil getting at? He was angry because he wanted him to get into a good school?

"Well, you told me if I wanted to get into any of those top schools, I'd have to write a killer essay."

Vincent's head began to spin. Everything around him became fuzzy.

"And, admit it," Neil continued, "probably with the exception of the ending, you thought the writing was great."

Nod.

"And, I know how much Vincent Kraver loves a good mystery."

Vincent shook his head. He couldn't believe what he was hearing. It made no sense, yet it was still happening. His son was murdering him.

"Of course, I'll have to edit it quite a bit. I might take out the whole peanut cookie, Kevin Larre revelation, crazy son part. That probably wouldn't look too good in a college essay. It's hard to get into Princeton, or any top school for that matter, with a criminal record, especially one with murder on it. I'd ask for your help editing, but you're usually busy, so I won't bother you about it."

Neil patted his dad's back and rose from his spot on the floor with a grunt. "Oh man. I should probably take it easy. I told Justin that he and his friends should do their worst without killing me or putting me in a coma. They certainly did a thorough job."

Walking back to the desk, Neil picked up the plate of cookies. "I guess I'll write a letter from another adoring fan who wanted to send you cookies. It's too bad Vincent Kraver forgot to read the ingredients before eating some." Neil popped another cookie in his mouth. "These really are delicious. I'll leave them in the kitchen so everyone can eat them."

Neil reached the door and turned once more to face Vincent before leaving the office. "Oh, and I'll make sure Susan doesn't eat too many of them. I know you're concerned about her weight."

The door closed, and Vincent was left lying on the floor with only a few moments of life remaining. He didn't know what to think about Neil's reason for doing what he did. At this point, did it really matter?

Vincent's body started convulsing in a desperate attempt to let him know it needed oxygen, as if he really needed to be told.

As the last sparks of life faded within Vincent, one last thought came into the writer's mind.

Of course Neil will get into Princeton. He is, after all, Vincent Kraver's son.

EPILOGUE

Mr. Thompson tapped his fingers on the shiny desk in front of him as he read over the paperwork. The walls of his office were covered in various degrees and recognitions earned over his many years of study.

"I was so sorry to hear about your father. He was a great man, and one hell of a writer."

"That he was," said Neil softly, offering a slight smile to show his appreciation of Mr. Thompson's condolences.

"And, the biography you wrote of him was very moving. He would have been very proud."

"Thank you, sir."

"Do you know what you would study if you were to be accepted here?"

"Not specifically yet," replied Neil. "However, I feel I have a lot of passion, much like my father, and when I finally choose my direction, I will do my very best to excel."

"That's good to know."

"I'd also like you to know that I fully intend to put all the money my father left me toward furthering my education. It's what I want, and I know it's what my father would want as well."

After studying Neil for a few minutes and looking over his application forms one more time, Mr. Thompson stood and reached out his hand toward Neil.

"Well, Neil Kraver, on behalf of the administration, I'd like to officially welcome you to Princeton. Congratulations, son."

DISCARD

Made in the USA
Lexington, KY
18 August 2010